Bailey's Pond

Mickey Stroda

ISBN: 1-931297-37-1

This book is dedicated to my children; Spencer, Sara and Steven. I love you guys.

Authors Note: My family and I DID live at Bailey's Pond in 1976 and I based my story on that time. While this book IS a work of fiction, many of the characters are based on real people and the towns of Mt. Pleasant and Batesville ARE real, as well as Bailey's Pond.

Bailey's Pond

Mickey Stroda

Prologue

The horror the small town of Mt. Pleasant, Arkansas had been experiencing for so long has been waiting; waiting for the time it could strike. It has been incubating in a pond outside of town, a pond known as Bailey's Pond. The evil minions protecting the evil have been at work readying themselves for it's coming.

This is the tale of two star-crossed lovers, Em and Chris, who get caught up in that horror. To save the life of their young daughter, they are forced to face the most horrible evil known to mankind. An evil older than time itself. An evil so horrible it hasn't even been *spoken* of for over twenty years.

Chapter 1

Black Eyes

Chris '96

"The evil started about twenty-five years ago," Chris began, his voice trembling slightly, as he forced himself to recall the events of that long ago night, "What I remember most are the snakes, Em; **lots** of snakes. The fish around the area were all dying, they were washing up on the shores of lakes and ponds everywhere because the population of snakes was continuing to grow at an alarming rate; forcing the fish out of the water, on to the shores to die. With the worst of it out by Bailey's Pond," he paused to take a sip of his soda, an old favorite of ours; Mt. Dew with M&M's dropped in it. "The town was failing fast, with people either dying or leaving. So many people died that summer in such a short period of time that a lot of the people left began to get scared and quite a few of them packed up and left the area, it was like a mass exodus. I guess a lot of people thought there was a sickness of some kind, like a plague or something, pretty soon there were very few people left in the area. It wasn't just the people dying that was frightening those who were left, it was the *way* they were dying. Snakes were not only biting anyone that even got near them, they seemed to be actually *searching* out the people to bite them. They were like rabid animals; searching, hunting, **attacking**! There were so many cases of snakebite in such a short period of time that the town council ordered ALL snakes to be hunted and killed, by any means necessary! And the spiders!" He shivered, "there were spiders everywhere you looked. Those damn big, hairy tarantulas your mom was always so fond of. I love your mom, but her fondness for spiders always gave me the creeps." Nobody who had ever known her had understood mom's fondness for the things. I suppose in a way they *are* pretty, but mostly, they're just *creepy*. "The spiders seemed to be much bigger that summer; getting at least four times bigger than they usually do and there was a whole lot more of 'em. Then one night, at a town council meeting that most of the town attended for some reason; the town meetings were not usually attended by very many people, but this one was, probably because everyone wanted to know what was being done about all the spiders and snakes in the area, Anyway, a stranger showed up at that particular meeting and told everyone there that he could explain what was going on, could explain *why* all kinds of strange things had been happening in the area, if they would give him the chance. He said he thought they were being punished by God, for some wrong done by them or maybe some of their ancestors; he wasn't sure which it was, but he told them he believed that to be the reason. He told them his…. Boss… wanted him to tell them that he could *solve* their problem **and** control the spiders and snakes that had been running wild for the past few months, for a price; *FOR A PRICE, Em*!!!! The people were so scared that they didn't even ask what the price would be or who the man's boss was; they just wanted to stop the plagues that had been visited on them for months now, for whatever reason. By the time they found out the price, *and* who the mans boss **really** was, it was too late to do anything to stop it. None of them even suspected that the black eyed mans boss was the one who had *started* the plague in the first place, so of course he would be able to solve the problem. And that man's boss has *nothing whatsoever* to do with God!! Just the opposite in my opinion. "

My mind was whirling with the realization that my fears had been justified. I wasn't losing my mind, or, if I *was*, it wasn't because I believed evil had taken over the entire area AND the man I loved. I found myself wondering just exactly WHAT I had gotten myself and my children into; I thought of turning and running from this place and the evil it contained, the danger it held, for anyone foolish enough to settle here; but I knew I couldn't leave Chris to face the danger alone any longer. I had been gone twenty years already, (NOT by choice, but gone nonetheless.) I *knew* I had to stay and help the man I had loved for most of my life, if there was any way I COULD help. He NEEDED me! And I needed him, though my need for him was for a completely different reason. From what he was telling me, I wasn't sure there was anything *anyone* could do.

"He was a strange looking man. About six feet tall, around one hundred and ninety five pounds, brown hair, dark complexion, and I swear Em, **BLACK EYES**! I couldn't stop looking at his *eyes*; it was like they were a magnet, drawing everyone's eyes to his. They seemed to radiate a ... force of some kind, which in a way they did, that's what I remember thinking at the time. I don't know how else to describe it. It was .... eerie, that's the only word I know that even comes close to describing it."

After pausing to light himself and I a cigarette, he continued, "Later, at home, when I tried to tell my mom that there was something 'bad', something evil about the man, she told me I was just being silly, and there was nothing to be afraid of, nothing at all. I *tried* to believe her, I *wanted* to believe her, but a part of me couldn't. Every time I'd think about those black eyes, I would feel a shiver go up my spine and the hair on the back of my neck would stand up." He shivered and said, "It STILL happens whenever I think of those damn black eyes!" He rubbed the back of his neck, as if the hair was standing up even now, just thinking about the mans eyes. "But I never said anything about it again, after that night, to my mom, *or* to anyone else. I knew she wouldn't believe me, any more than she had believed me that first night; and if I couldn't even get my own mother to believe what I was saying, why should I think anyone else would. So I kept it to myself."

I said "It *is* a parent's job to try to calm their child's fears, Chris. I'm sure she didn't mean to just blow you off like that. Maybe she just didn't want you to be afraid. I believe I probably would have told any of my children pretty much the same thing, but it wouldn't be because I didn't believe them, it would be because I was trying to keep them calm. I would hope they could understand what I was trying to do and not think as you did that night with your mom. I don't blame you though, I suppose I never really thought about how my kids would react if I did say something like that to them."

"I know she was only trying to soothe me Em, to make it so I wouldn't be so afraid, but it really bothered me that she didn't believe me. I'm just sorry it turned out I was RIGHT!!"

Shivering, even though the temperature was eighty seven degrees on the patio; I told him I had to agree with him on that one. Even now, with him telling me of the evil that had existed for so many years in this small pleasant town, the evil that had permeated throughout the whole area; as well as all the strange things I myself had witnessed since my return, I still found myself having a hard time believing it all. Believing that there was such immense evil taking over the area, and Lord only knows what plans it had for the future, for the people in this area, as well as the rest of the country; who knows, maybe even the entire world.

If anyone from outside the affected area had been told, they would have thought everyone in the entire area had gone insane, at least those few who were still able to think for themselves, even if only a little bit. It isn't something that people want or for that matter are even *ready*, to believe; the fact that evil DOES exist among us and can show up in the least likely of places. Before my return to Mt. Pleasant, if anyone had told me *any* of the strange and unusual things Chris was telling me now, I would have thought they had lost their minds. Now, after living here and having experienced even a small measure of the evil first-hand, I was ready to believe anything was possible. No, now I *knew* anything was possible.

God, it's amazing how much things can change in such a short space of time. Less than a year ago I had no idea that evil such as this even existed; let alone that normal, everyday people, like Chris and the other people in Mt. Pleasant and the surrounding area, were being forced to live with it; as the people in this area had been forced to do for twenty-five years.

Chris broke into my thoughts, reaching to take my hand in his, "What are you thinking right now Em?"

I told him.

Chapter 2

Starting Over

Em '96

"I sold my latest book today guys," I told my kids as I walked in the house. "My agent and publisher were thrilled!"

"Oh mom, that's great!!" said my sixteen year old daughter, Chloe, "But I thought Emily said it might be a while. At least until you got closer to finishing it." Her twin brother Jake jr. (who we called JJ), shook his head, as if to agree with her.

"It *IS* finished. I finished it last weekend?" I flopped down on the couch, bone tired. "Meeting with agents, publishers and all the other people you have to see to get a book published sure takes a lot out of you. It's always amazed me how much work it is to get a book published," I shook my head, thinking of all the work that went into getting even one book published. "To most people I'm sure the writing seems like the hard part, but that's actually the easy part for me, at least compared to the work you have to go through to get it published."

"But why didn't you *tell* us it was finished?"

"I wanted to surprise you," I could tell by the looks on their faces that I had definitely surprised them. "Wait until I tell you the amount of money that was offered in the contract Emily showed me today. She was so happy, because it meant her commission was even more than it has been on my previous books."

"It was actually *more* than last time, even?" Joe, my thirteen year old asked, excitedly.

"Oh Yeah, two more zeros, to be exact."

""WOW!!"

"No wonder Em was thrilled. You're moving up Mom. It's hard to believe anyone can make that much money for writing a book. But, you're worth it and the publishers finally realize it."

"That's a **lot** of money. What *shall* we do with it all??" Chloe said, doing her best imitation of Mrs. Thurston Howell III from Gilligan's Island.

"Put most of it in the bank, as usual." I didn't tell JJ and Chloe I was also planning to buy each of them a car for their sixteenth birthday's, which were coming up soon. *That* would be their next surprise. I really enjoyed doing whatever I could to make my children happy and the money from the sale of my books helped me to do that.

"Mommy! Mommy!! I'm so glad you're finally home!! I miss you so-o-o much when you're not here!" Kat, my youngest, at five, came running into the room and jumped on me, hugging me and kissing me all over the face. It broke the tension and we all laughed at her antics.

"We'll talk about all this later," I said to the other three, over the top of Kat's head.

"OK, mom, we'll go in and start supper," Chloe said as she and her brothers headed for the kitchen. I was glad they weren't like a lot of kids their age I had heard as well as read about; that would never even *THINK* of volunteering to help their parents. Or, for that matter, do anything around the house at all. They had always been a big help to me, but since their father's death almost thirteen years earlier, it seemed they had gone out of their way to help even more; as if they knew I would not have been able to do everything by myself.

"They're good kids, thank goodness. I really got lucky with them," I said aloud to myself as I scooped Kat up and headed for the bathroom to take a nice hot bath that I hoped would help to ease the tension in my muscles; my shoulders were in knots and my legs were beginning to cramp. I knew supper wouldn't be ready for about an hour so I had plenty of time to relax in a hot bath. **If** having a five year old sitting at the vanity next to the tub, chattering nonsensically the whole time, could be called relaxing. Even though I didn't have the slightest idea what she was talking about most of the time, I did enjoy the time we got to spend together, she made me laugh a lot, which helped to ease any tension I happened to be feeling.

After I had gotten dressed and was attempting to brush my long, thick hair, Kat decided she wanted to help her brothers and sister with supper, so she ran downstairs to the kitchen. Left alone with my thoughts, I thought for probably the hundred thousandth time how fortunate we were that about three months after Joseph was born in 1983, the kids' father had decided to up the insurance on he and I, and also insure the kids as well. He had ours both upped to seven hundred and fifty thousand dollars each, with each of the kids being insured for two hundred and fifty thousand dollars each. He said you can never be *too* careful, *too* loved or *too* insured. He also told me he wanted to make sure that if anything ever happened to him, (God forbid!) the kids and I would be well provided for.

I remember when he had brought up the idea of more insurance, he and I had started a running joke about killing the other one off and retiring on the insurance money; the kids thought it was morbid but they knew we were only joking. Less than a year later, he was killed in a horrible plane crash. I remember wondering if maybe he'd had some kind of premonition, or was psychic or something. . After everything was settled, with our insurance company as well as the airline's insurance company, which took about a year; the kids and I had a little over a million and a half in the bank. It was hard, even now, for any of us to imagine we really had that much money in the bank. I had put two hundred fifty thousand each into three savings accounts for the kids when they reached the age of twenty one, with the stipulation that if they wanted to go to college before they reached that age, the tuition could come out of their personal account. That wouldn't affect the initial deposit much, if at all, because the interest alone should be enough to cover the costs of college. Thank God, I had married a man who planned ahead.

By the time Kat was three years old I had made enough money from the sale of my books that I was able to also put two hundred and fifty thousand into an account for her, so all four of my kids were well provided for. It made me so happy to be able to give each of them a nest egg to begin building their futures on.

When Kat came bursting into my room I was still absent mindedly brushing my hair, "MOMMY!! MOMMY!! It's time to eat now, let's go, Mommy, let's go! I'm hungry!! Aren't you hungry Mommy? I sure am, I'm starving! I haven't had anything to eat since lunch and it wasn't enough!"

Kat was constantly hungry as well as always being excited and happy, no matter what had happened to her during the day. The only thing I could recall that had ever even come close to bringing her down from the clouds she seemed to constantly be in was if we talked about her father, so the other kids and I didn't talk about him, at least *not* where she could hear us. Even though she had never met him, she did know a few things I'd told her about him and she knew his name, which was Chris. When the other kids and I came home at the end of our days, her abundance of energy and happiness seemed to be able to drain out of us any bad feelings we had brought home. Kat grabbed my arm and led me to the dining room for supper.

After we had cleaned off the table, straightened up the kitchen and gotten the dishes washed, the kids and I made some popcorn and went to the family room to watch television for a while. At eight o'clock I took Kat upstairs so she could take a bath and brush her teeth. I read her a story after I tucked her in, which I tried to do every night, as I had also done with the other three; by nine o'clock she was sound asleep. It was time to go down and talk to the other kids now, they were as excited about the sale of my newest book as I was. They had been supportive of me since I first began writing, almost ten years ago. It had taken me a while to get my first book published, it was the first in a series about a nun that liked to help the police investigate and solve crimes they were having problems with. After it came out, I was flooded with offers from other publishers, trying to entice me away from the company that had published my first book. I decided to stay with the first company though because they had been more than fair with their offer on my first book. I was glad now I had chosen to remain with them.

Turning out the light in Kat's room, I started downstairs. As I was going down the stairs I heard the phone ringing. "Mom, it's for you," I heard Jake yell down the hall, "Sorry, I forgot Kat's trying to sleep," he said, covering the mouthpiece with his hand as I took the phone from him.

I smiled and he knew he had been forgiven, "Hello," I spoke into the receiver, about to get a big surprise of my own.

"Em! Long time no see!"

"Chris? Chris Dixon? I can't believe it! I was just thinking about you! God, we haven't seen each other in…. how long now?"

"Almost six years Em. It's been a while. It was Las Vegas, 1990, remember?" I knew exactly when it was we had seen each other last and where. How *could* I ever forget? I myself had just been thinking about Vegas, Kat and him, I thought as I felt my face turning red. "I was just down by my dock, working on my houseboat and began thinking about you, which, by the way, I do quite often. Think of you I mean, not work on the houseboat." He laughed as he tried to explain what he had meant, finally giving up, "Anyway back to the reason I called, I got to wondering what you'd been up to for the last few years, so I thought I would call and find out how you've been and what you have been up to lately. How are those three monsters of yours doing?" He joked.

His question touched a chord in me, (he still believed I only had three children), it brought back the realization that I had never told him about Kat, or that *he* was her father. I had been meaning to tell him for years, but something else always came up or something happened to stop me. As the years passed, I just couldn't seem to get up enough nerve to tell him, 'Because you're worried how he will react to the news, and about how he will react to the fact that you *haven't* told him about Kat in all this time, when you *know* he has the right to know,' I told myself silently. Which was true, the last time we had seen each other, in Vegas, he had made it perfectly clear to me that he already had three children and he didn't want, or *need* any more. I *was* kind of worried that he would be angry with me, or worse yet, that he wouldn't accept her.

His call had come at precisely the right time, I had just finished my latest book, the kids were all out of school for the summer, and there was no time like the present. This, however was the kind of news you tell someone face-to-face, not on the phone, so I planned to ask him if the kids and I could come to Arkansas for a visit soon.

"They're fine Chris, and what about those hooligans of yours, what have they been up to? Have they been staying out of trouble?" I joked with him. Ever since we'd had kids, whenever we talked we joked back and forth about them. Each calling the others' names like monster, hooligan or a variety of other names along those lines.

We talked for about half an hour longer and just before we hung up I said, "Chris, if it's alright with my kids, would you mind if we came for a visit sometime soon."

"Of course Em. You can come down here anytime you want. I would love to see you again, and I am really looking forward to meeting those monsters of yours," He laughed and I wondered if he would be so eager to see me if he knew what I was going to tell him, what I hadn't told him, for over five years. "I'm sure the kids will all get along great Em."

"Thanks Chris, that means a lot to me. I'll let you know in the next few days what we decide. I just hope you guys are ready for the invasion," I joked. 'I also hope you're ready for the news I'm going to give you," I thought to myself.

"Oh, we can handle it, I'm sure." He laughed, "I can't wait to see you again Em. I'll talk to you soon. Bye, for now."

"Later Chris." Now all I had to do was tell the kids my plan and hope they agreed to go.

"Mom, I think that's a GREAT idea!" This from Chloe, "Kat will be so happy that she will finally get to know her dad! And you know I have always wanted to meet the man you have talked about constantly all my life. I swear, I know more about him than I do my all my ex boyfriends put together!!" She laughed. I didn't think I had talked about Chris that much, but when she said that, it made me realize that I had told her and her brothers just about everything about the time my family had spent in Mt. Pleasant in nineteen seventy six and seven.

"I LOVE IT!!" JJ said. He had always been the adventurous type and was usually ready to go anywhere. He really enjoyed seeing new places and meeting new people. He was so much like his father in that respect.

Joe was the only one with any reservations and the other two soon talked him out of those. By the time they were done talking to him he could hardly wait to get to Arkansas. "I'm glad for Kat, I know it will make her happy to meet him after all this time," Joe said to me.

By the time we went to bed we had decided we would leave early Sunday morning so we would arrive at Chris' early that evening. I called Chris the next day to let him know we would be there sometime before supper on Sunday, if that was alright with him. I called on a Wednesday so that gave him and his kids a little time to get ready for the invasion of five people that was going to hit them, as well as giving my kids and I enough time to get things packed and ready for the trip.

Chris was thrilled, "My kids are really looking forward to finally meeting the woman that I have, as they put it, 'gone on about' for years."

"Chloe said pretty much the same thing to me last night when I had brought the subject of coming to visit you up," I told him about the conversation my kids and I had the previous evening, we laughed about it and both said we were really looking forward to seeing each other again so we could catch up on what had been going on in each other's lives for the past few years. Was he ever in for a shock, I could only hope he would be able to forgive me for not having told him about Kat for all this time.

Chapter 3

The First Move

Em '76

Nineteen seventy six, the year of so many important events. On top of being the year of our country's Bi Centennial, this was a landmark year for me as well; it was the year of my fifteenth birthday, the year of my first date, the year of my first fight that *wasn't* with my sisters, the year my parents decided to pull up roots our family had been putting down for the last fifteen years, and the year I would meet the man I would love for the rest of my life. Moving, after having spent the first fifteen years of my life in one place was a very frightening idea for me, but I knew I would be able to deal with it, and it wasn't as if I had a choice about it or anything like that. Our parents had not asked my sister's opinions, or mine for that matter, about the move, they just decided it was the best thing for all of us. I suppose they were right, with all the problems our family had been facing in the last year or so.

In the past year, my father had gotten laid off from a job he had held for almost twenty years and couldn't seem to find another one in the area that would support a family of six; my sister Jaicie had been getting in trouble with the law because she had started hanging around with the wrong crowd and our mom and dad had been arguing due to a lack of money. Our parents really loved each other and up until that time had seldom disagreed, which made it especially hard for us to see them argue. (Even with everything else that had been going on over the past year, I think the arguing was the hardest thing for my sister's and I to handle.) Unemployment just wasn't covering the needs of a family of six so we hardly ever had enough food, the utility bills were getting more and more delinquent, with creditors calling so often we had to get the phone taken out. (Not that we would have had it for much longer anyway, because we couldn't afford to pay the phone bill.) My grandmother, Mom's mother, who lived across town from us, helped as much as she could, but since she had a tendency to help us even to the point of her having to do without, mom and dad didn't let her help as much as she wanted to.

Even though dad and my older sister Ren and I all three went hunting in the winter, selling the pelts of the animals we caught, (my family eating the meat, YUCK!! We weren't much for meat eating), and all of us kids and dad went fishing in the summer, there was still never enough money or food to go around. I remember thinking at the time that I hoped the rest of my life would go better than the past year had.

So, the decision to move was NOT something my sister's and I would have fought, even if we had been able to. We were tired of not having enough food, never enough money to get even *some* of the things our friends had and worst of all, the sound of our parent's fighting in the night.

My dad planned to go on to Arkansas ahead of the family to start his new job and hopefully, find a place for us to live. After he left he called us at grandmas house at least twice a week, to let us know how his new job was going and to keep us updated on the house hunting.

Finally, two months after he left, my mom decided that she was sick and tired of having the family split up and the next time he called, she said, "The kids and I are coming down Johnny, I'm tired of our family being separated like it has for the past few months."

"But, hon, you know I still haven't found a place for us to live. I'm still staying at your brothers house here, you know that."

"I know and I don't care whether we have a house to live in or not. I did *not* marry you just so we could both be living like we were single; as long as we're all together that is all that matters to me. I want us to be a family again." So, without a home to live in, or even the prospect of one in the near future, we packed up and moved to Arkansas.

A few years earlier, when my dad had still had his job, he and my mom had bought a cab-over camper, one of those that are hauled on the back of a pickup truck, we packed only what we absolutely had to have in it and a small trailer that we pulled along behind the truck and camper. When we got to Arkansas, we pulled the truck into my uncle's yard, unhooked the camper right next to his house and set up housekeeping.

Chapter 4

The Face Of Evil

Chris '96

After I told him what I had been thinking, Chris continued telling me about the town meeting and the repercussions it had on the people in the area so long ago; the effect it was *still* having. I could tell it bothered him to talk about it, but he forced himself to go on with the story, knowing it had to finally be told. He *had* to get it off his chest, he was afraid if he didn't tell someone, he would lose his mind.

"Like I said, after that night I didn't mention my feelings about that man again to my mom, *or* anyone else. I kept an eye on him though believe me; a *very close* eye on him," Chris paused to light us both another cigarette, then continued, "I knew nobody was going to believe a kid my age if I told them my feelings, so I just kept all of it to myself and continued to watch him." He sighed, as he remembered not being able to tell anybody what was going on, what he believed was going to happen to all of them if they let the black eyed man have his way. Which was exactly what they *did* plan on doing, they wanted to rid themselves of the spiders and snakes, no matter what it cost them.

"That must have been hard for you, being that frightened and not being able to tell anybody your suspicions. I can't even imagine how it would make me feel if I was ever placed in that position." As I said this to him, I placed my hand on his knee.

He covered my hand with his, "Even though I'm so sorry you and your children had to get mixed up in this, I don't know how I could have continued to face this evil alone and I am really glad you guys are here now, to support me and if you can to help."

"I am really happy to be here Chris and I hope I can help you in some way, even though I don't know what, if anything I can help with as well as the fact that I *AM* more afraid than I have ever been in my entire life. I'm scared out of my wits, in fact!" We both laughed and it helped to ease the tension his story, and the evil, was causing.

He continued with his tale of terror, "That was the strangest town meeting I ever went to Em. After listening to that man outline the plans he and his boss had for our town, I couldn't believe no-one else could figure out that what he was proposing could only mean one thing for our town and the people in it. Terror, with a **_CAPITAL T_**!! I was afraid, and I was only a *child*. I couldn't understand why nobody else was frightened. It seemed like nobody else there even *suspected* what he was planning."

"I wonder why you were the only one there that saw him for what he really was and that what he was planning wouldn't help anyone but him, and his boss. Was everybody else at the meeting asleep, or just plain stupid?"

"Asleep; or in a daze anyway. At least that's what it looked like to me. By the time that meeting was over they didn't seem to have any will of their own. They seemed only to be able to do what the black eyed man suggested they do."

"But why didn't whatever it was affect you?"

"I've been working on that one since the night I first met that man. I think I may have come up with a reason for it but I need just a little more time to make absolutely sure."

"Well, I just hope you're right."

"I'm about ninety-five percent certain I am, but it's that other five percent that kinda scares me. I'll let you know what I've come up with in a day or two, I should have it figured out by then. Ok?"

"Alright. What exactly have you figured out about his 'proposition', or whatever you'd call it?"

"All I could uncover for sure, was that it had to do with putting…… something…. an evil…. In Bailey's Pond."

"Are you telling me that my family and I lived *right **next*** to the evil when we lived there!?!? Almost on top of it?? That it was *IN THE POND* next to our house*???*" My voice cracked, squeaking with the immense terror that was filling me, threatening to break free. Chris caught me just as my knees buckled.

Chapter 5

New Beginnings

Both '96

As we pulled in to Chris' driveway I could feel the butterflies that were flying around in my stomach threatening to fly out my mouth. I was worried about his reaction when he found out about Kat, wondering if he would be *very* angry at me. I knew he would be angry, to some extent, I would be too, if the shoe had been on the other foot, the roles reversed; but I hoped he would be able to forgive me. Up to now, the only ones who knew the whole truth about Kat's paternity were my three other children and I, all Kat knew was her father's name.

Chris and his family were waiting for us on the wrap around porch that went three quarters of the way around the house. Behind the house was a large brick patio that would soon become one of my favorite places to sit and think.

I could see the questioning look in Chris' eyes when he saw Kat as we got out of the car. I was sure he was probably wondering whose child she was and why we would bring someone else's child with us on vacation. I know that was exactly what I would be thinking if I were in his place. The butterflies from my stomach had worked their way up to my throat by now.

Luckily, Chris had a large house and after getting everything out of the car we found rooms for all of us and got settled in. My two sons and Chris' son, Chris jr. who was called CJ to avoid confusion, were in the finished basement bedrooms, Chloe in CJ's room, Kat in one of the guest rooms with me in a room with her on one side and Chris on the other, his daughter's stayed in their own rooms. It was quite a madhouse, with everyone laughing and joking with each other. Chris had been right, our children got along great, they acted like they had known each other for years. Soon, when things began to settle down and the kids had all found something to do, Chris and I walked out to the gazebo. As we sat on a bench he looked at me expectantly. 'Here goes!' I thought silently to myself. 'D-Day!' "I know, you want me to tell you about Kat."

"Yes, at first I was kind of wondering whose child she was, and why in the world you would bring someone else's child with you; but she's yours, isn't she Em."

"I don't know any other way to say this Chris except to just say it flat out; yes, she's mine, but not *just* mine, she's *ours*. Remember Vegas, in 1990." I prepared myself for the onslaught of surprise, anger and shock, *all* of which I was sure he would be feeling.

Luckily he was sitting down when I dropped the bombshell on him, "Why Em? Why didn't you ever tell me? You could have, ***should have*** told me."

"I know Chris, and I'm so sorry I didn't. But in Vegas you let me know in no uncertain terms that you had enough children and weren't interested in ever having any more. Two months later, when I found out I was pregnant, I was afraid of what you would say if I told you; then, as time passed I didn't seem to be able to bring myself to tell you. I know I should have told you and I know it was wrong of me not to, but I can't change that now. All I can do is hope you're not *too* upset with me," I stood up and looked out over the lake behind the gazebo, "Oh, by the way, Kat *doesn't* know. All I've ever told her about her father is his name," I sighed, "I decided when you called that I was going to tell you, but I didn't really want to break news like this over the phone, so I came up with the idea that I would come here and tell you face to face; then *together*, we could finally introduce Kat to her father, as well as her father to her. We can tell her tomorrow, if you want."

Chris stood up to put his arms around me and said, " I'd like that very much Em. I'm glad you didn't tell me over the phone; news like this *is* something that needs to be told when you are with the person that is to be told, isn't it? How do you think she'll react to it?"

"Well, she's waited five years to meet her father, and she seemed to take to you right off so I'm sure she'll be thrilled. Don't worry, she'll love you, I know she will."

"I hope so. I'm a little nervous. God, another daughter." He smiled as he said it, then he hugged me, so I knew he wasn't too upset about the idea.

"Dad, Em, supper," Chris' daughter Kim hollered out to the gazebo from the patio. Chris' place was beautiful and I was glad we had decided to come here so I could tell him, as well as to visit with him and his children. He had bought an old farmhouse that sat on seventy acres and fixed it up. From the gazebo you could see the horses and sheep in the pasture, a building that had once been slave quarters and a beautiful lake that seemed to stretch on forever with a long dock that had a boathouse attached which housed the two boats Chris had. One of them was an old beater that he had bought so he and his son, CJ, could fix it up together. The houseboat he had been working on when he decided to call me was tied to the dock. It was so peaceful and quiet here, reminding me a lot of when my family had moved to Bailey's Pond all those years ago.

I had never met a man that enjoyed being with his children as much as Chris did. He spent as much time as he could with each of them, separately as well as together; managing his time so he could do something special with each. Something the child was interested in, it didn't matter to Chris if he found it interesting or not; it was enough for him that he was spending time with them and he did all he could to make the time he spent with each, 'quality time'. They appreciated the effort he put into keeping the family happy, loving and together. They knew he loved them above all else and returned those feelings. The loving family he had helped create and was now a part of, was very different than the family he had grown up in. The only similarity to it was that he was a single parent, as his mom had been; though this was not a choice on Chris' part, as it had been for his mother and father.

Chris' childhood had not been an easy one for him, it would have been hard on any child. His mom and dad had divorced when he was a baby and he had ended up living with his mom, who soon became an alcoholic. The relationship he had with his mother was a strange one, with him having to take over the role of parent, even though he was the child, because *someone* had to be responsible and his mom's 'illness' made it impossible for her to be the responsible one. Chris didn't really mind, probably because at that age he didn't know that, as a child, he shouldn't have had to be so responsible; he should have been allowed to be a child, but fate seemed to have chosen a very different path for him.

A child *isn't* meant to be an adult. If they had been, they wouldn't have been born babies, they would have been born fully grown. Chris knew none of this as a child though it probably wouldn't have made any difference if he had, he loved his mom very much and even though, deep inside, he knew she was sick, he never held any of it against her. Their home life was well known in the small town, so growing up Chris occasionally got into fights with some of the other kids, who, as children sometimes tend to do, often made rude comments about his moms *condition*. He couldn't stand it when *anyone* said bad things about his mom, although, at times, he himself **thought** many of the things the others were saying. He loved her and felt it was his duty to protect her, which he did, to the best of his ability.

Although over the years his mom didn't change, remained an alcoholic, slowly getting worse as time went by; Chris *did* change. He came to realize that it's supposed to be the parent who takes on the responsibilities of the family, good or bad, *not* the child. He vowed to himself that when he had a family, (if he ever did), he would be a loving father that shouldered the responsibility. He would give his children *only* the responsibilities they *should* have, and only as much as they could handle, *nothing more*. He knew they would have to deal with some things on their own, but he was determined to help them as much as he could. They would have to deal with responsibility soon enough in their lives, as adults. He kept the vow he had made to himself all those years ago and had three happy, well adjusted children; and a very happy, loving family. I was proud of him.

I finally realized Chris had his hand on my shoulder and was gently shaking me to get my attention, I turned to him, "Damn woman, where were you? Lost in the ozone? It's time to go in to supper. We better hurry up and get some food before those monsters of ours eat it all," he joked.

'Sorry, I was lost in my thoughts, again." I smiled as I said this because I had always had a tendency to lose myself in my thoughts for as long as I could remember. From the look on his face he remembered too.

"Yeah, I seem to remember that you sometimes zone out. Where do you go when you do that anyway? I always have been curious about that. Think you'll eve let me in on it?" He grinned.

Walking across the back patio, we could see the entire kitchen and through the large archway that led into the dining room. All of our children were hustling to put the finishing touches on supper, and while Kat wasn't really much help at five, she *did* try. None of the others seemed to mind her being constantly underfoot, which kind of surprised me with Chris' kids because they hadn't been used to having a little one around until my children and I had come to visit. They *must* be well adjusted, to have been able to adapt to having us invade their lives as quickly as they seemed to be doing. I don't know of many teens who would have welcomed five strangers into their lives and home as readily as Kim, CJ and Kari had. Chris had every right to be proud of his children and I knew he was.

Chapter 6

Batesville

Em '76

The transition of living on a farm to all six of us in a small camper was difficult, but my aunt and uncle had been through their share of hard times before and they were very good to us. They let us stay in the house if we needed, (like when it stormed), let us do our laundry in the house as well as allowing mom to cook in their kitchen sometimes, which she really appreciated. Their help and understanding did a lot to make the transition easier for all of us. Luckily, we would only have to stay in the camper for three months, because it was just **way** too small a place for a family of six to be forced to live.

As you walked in the door of the camper, straight ahead was the bed that went over the cab of the truck, where my mom and dad slept, with Karli between them; to your left was the table, which at night converted into a bed for my sister Rennie (Ren) and I, above the table/bed was a cabinet that folded down into another bed for our younger sister Jaicie (Jace). The bathroom, which contained a shower and toilet was just inside the door to the right, walking straight ahead you would see the sink and small refrigerator on your right, the stove was to the left. Being so small, it was definitely *not* someplace a family should be *living* for any extended period of time.

Even though our lives had changed dramatically in a very short period of time, my sister's and I seemed to adapt pretty quick. We treated life as an adventure and simply acted like our family was on an extended camping trip, instead of actually living in the camper. Later in life, when I looked back on our time in Batesville, I realized that while our outlook may have been childish, it was probably the reason we were able to cope with it as well as we did. We also had **GREAT** neighbors, which helped a lot.

We quickly made friends with the other kids our age in the neighborhood and within a week my older sister, Ren and our younger sister Jace and I had gotten enrolled in school, four weeks into the spring semester. The youngest, Karli, was only four so she couldn't go to school yet. Arkansas was, however, one of the few states that would allow her to go to school the next fall, even though she wouldn't be five until about three weeks into the semester. When we had lived in Kansas, she would have had to wait until she was almost six before she could have gone to school, because her birthday was three days *after* the cut off date the state used to determine when children could go to school. She could hardly wait until the next fall, when she would actually get to go to school with the rest of us.

Going to a new school was a little scary at first, but once we realized a school is a school no matter where it's at, my sister's and I settled in nicely. The friends we'd made from the neighborhood did everything they could to help my sister's and I adjust. I was lucky and ended up with most of my classes with two of them, so that made it easier for me.

I was nearing the end of my freshman year and while I had never really liked the school I had attended all my life up to then, I enjoyed the time I spent there. I think it was probably because the school I had attended before then had **really** pushed us to learn so I was way ahead of the rest of the class in most subjects. The only class I had a problem with was math, which had been a weak spot for me throughout my school years (and would continue to be a problem for me for quite a few years to come). Overall though, I did well in my new surroundings. Rennie, being a junior, had been having a harder time adjusting to having to leave behind all the friends she'd had for so long. I believe the move was harder for her than for any of the rest of us, but she had always done well in school, gotten good grades and she continued to do so. Jaicie was thirteen and in the seventh grade, she didn't really care one way or the other *where* she went to school, she just hated the fact that she was made to go *at all*. By the time she had reached the fourth grade, she had finally come to the conclusion that she *DID* have to go to school and she began settling down and making good grades; whether she liked it or not.

Home life began to get more settled, with my sister's and I having friends to hang out with. Paul and Sharee Johnson lived across the street to the East, Terry and Talia, the Kyler twins, lived just to the East of them. My favorite was Jimmy Dean, who lived one and a half blocks North up the street.

Every day after school we would all get together and find something to do. Usually we ended up playing ball in the empty lot to the South of us. None of us could have ever claimed to be Babe Ruth or Hank Aaron but we had a lot of fun playing. Every evening, when it would get close to suppertime, we could all hear Jimmy Dean's mom calling, "Jimmy De-e-E-Ean, Jimmy De-e-E-Ean!" Don't get me wrong, she was a very sweet woman and I loved her to death, but when she called for her son, it was a real kick. Of course none of us ever said anything about it because it seemed to embarrass Jimmy Dean.

I was sent to the principals office once during the time I went to school in Batesville. All because some girl had decided that I was looking at her boyfriend too much; I wasn't, but that didn't stop her from believing that I was. She started a fight with me right after school one day because of it. It turned out to be a four hit fight, she hit me once, I hit her twice and then she hit the ground. We both ended up with a fat lip, with her also having a black eye from the second time I had hit her; we also both ended up in the principals office. I got lucky and ended up with only two days of detention; but because that wasn't the first time the girl had started a fight and she had already been in detention for fighting, she got suspended from school for two weeks, then when she told the principal she didn't think she deserved to be suspended for so long, he added two weeks of detention added on top of it. She would have been better off if she had just kept her mouth shut.

One day when I didn't feel like being in school, I picked up my books after fourth hour and just walked out of the school. I had never done anything like that before so I was kind of scared I would get caught. I spent the morning wandering around town, window shopping; then just as I was beginning to wonder where, as well as *how* I was going to eat lunch, my Uncle drove by and I DID get caught. He promised he would never tell my parents he had caught me skipping school *if* I promised him it would never happen again, then he told me he would take me to lunch. I promised him it wouldn't and we went to eat lunch.

We spent the rest of the day together at the clinic he worked in, I helped him get things ready for an inspector that was to be coming the next day. As far as I know, he never *did* tell my parents how we had spent that day; and I never again skipped out of school without my parents knowing about it. We both kept the promises we made to each other that day.

My mom and dad spent the time we lived in the camper searching for a place for us to live that would be both big enough for all of us *and* wouldn't cost an arm and a leg to rent. About three months after Mom and us kids arrived in Batesville, Dad came home smiling, excited with the news that he had found a huge farmhouse for us just outside a small town named Mt. Pleasant.

He told us that it had five bedrooms, two of which were in the finished basement, (which meant that each of us girls would have a room of our own, something we'd never had before), two and a half baths, a huge kitchen, family room and dining room; a den for him and even a small pond on the property, just to the North of the house. He said another great thing was that it was only about thirty minutes from where he worked so he wouldn't have to get up at three in the morning to get to work. He said the best thing about it in his opinion though, was the rent, which was only a hundred and seventy five dollars a month. My mom couldn't understand why it was so inexpensive, but said she wasn't going to look a gift horse in the mouth; she was always coming up with an old saying of some kind for every situation; a habit of hers that had always driven me up the wall. Dad went on describing the house to us and said the place even had a name, 'Bailey's Pond'.

Chapter 7

Evil Lives

Chris '96

"Em! Em!!" I could hear Chris' voice, but it sounded like he was either talking to me from far away, or through a fan, "Are you OK?" He asked as he helped me sit up.

"OKAY!?! Of course I'm *NOT OKAY*!! I just found out that when I was fifteen years old my family lived practically right on top of probably the worst evil that's ever existed, for over a year; nobody told us, and you ask me if I'm OKAY!?!? Would you be OKAY!?!? I think NOT!! I don't know anyone who would be OKAY with that!" I knew I was rambling but what he'd just told me had blown my mind.

"I'm sorry hon, but at the time I still wasn't sure about it. I didn't know what, if anything, was in that damn pond and I didn't want to sound like a nut, running around saying I thought evil was going to take over the people in the area. I don't think anyone would have believed me even if I had told them my suspicions back then. Em, honey, I'm so sorry."

I felt terrible for going off on him like that, but it had been a hell of a shock finding out, that not only does evil exist, it had been right next to me for over a year. I could hear my mother's voice in my head, with another one of her annoying old sayings; 'Don't kill the messenger just because you don't like the message' and I knew it applied in this case. I Put my arms around Chris and lay my head on his shoulder, "I'm sorry for going off on you like that, but you have to admit that finding out my family and I lived so close to the source of the evil came as quite a shock. I hope you can forgive me for wiggin' out on you."

"*Me* forgive *you*? I was hoping *you'd* forgive *me* for not telling you all this twenty years ago. Maybe I *should* have told you, *and* your family even if I didn't tell anyone else; even if I *wasn't* a hundred percent sure about any of it," He said softly as he held me and stroked my back. It helped calm me.

"Of course I forgive you. Like you said, it wasn't as if you knew anything for sure. It was all still just guesswork at the time. And besides, most of the members of my family probably *would* have thought you had lost your mind if you had told us all of this back then." He relaxed, when I smiled as I said it, "OK, I'm feeling better now, maybe you should go on with the story."

"You sure you're up to it right now? Maybe you need a little time to think about everything I've told you so far. I can always pick up where I left off in the morning."

"You're right, maybe we should sleep on it tonight then start fresh in the morning. I'm still a little shook up about what I just found out and since it's not like this is something a person will **ever** be *prepared* to hear, I'm sure morning will be soon enough. Maybe a good nights sleep will help me digest what I've already heard and the extra time might help me to be able to absorb the rest of it. But remember Chris, I need to know *everything* you know about it so I can know *exactly* what we're facing."

"I know and I'm prepared to tell you everything Em, at least al that I've been able to figure out about what's been happening here since that man first came to town. I will even let you know the things I merely *suspect*, because if you are going to be involved in this mess, you need to know absolutely everything."

After breakfast the next morning Chris and I went down to the dock and sat with our feet dangling in the water, "Now where did I leave off? Oh yeah, like I was saying last night, it has to do with that black eyed man putting some kind of evil into Bailey's Pond. I still don't know exactly *what* it is, but from what I've been able to gather from the town meetings I've attended over the years I think that whatever it is, it needed the water to *incubate in*, or something. At least that's what I believe the people have been saying."

"My God, evil waiting to be born, in a little pond in the middle of Nowheresville, Arkansas. Well, they couldn't have picked a better place, that's for sure. Even if people *did* believe in evil, which I'm sure most don't, that's the last place they'd ever think to look."

"I believe that's exactly what the black eyed man had already decided before he even thought of approaching the town council for the first time. He had it all planned out when he came to that council meeting. He made sure he could answer the questions they would ask, or at the very least, that he could dance around the questions he didn't want to answer."

"So, when is it going to hatch, or be born, or whatever the hell it is that thing is supposed to do?"

"I'm not completely sure, but at the last town meeting I heard the black eyed man talking to some of the council members. He told them the 'Master' was ready to be born and that it should be happening any time now. That was two weeks ago."

"The 'Master'? It sounds even worse when you say it that way. Any time now, huh? That may mean we don't have much time left to deal with it, if any."

"I know. I even argued with myself about just grabbing the kids and haulin' ass out of here. I debated with myself about that for quite some time, then finally decided to discuss it with the kids, and we came to the conclusion that maybe we were the only ones who could stop it. That was before you and the kids got here, now that I have you here to help me maybe we will be able to stop it before it can spread any farther than Mt. Pleasant."

"I hope we can, Chris, It would be awful if we couldn't," I shivered, "I don't even want to *think* about that happening." The thought of the evil that was spreading through the area reaching any further than it was already was almost more than I could bear to think about. "Frankly Chris, that thought scares the hell out of me."

"Me too, Em. As a matter of fact, that thought has been what's pushed me to work harder that ever to fight this thing, especially since I first heard two weeks ago that at any time now it is getting ready to hatch or be born or whatever the hell it's going to do. So far, you and I and the kids, all seven of ours anyway, seem to be the only ones I can find around here that are immune to it's power."

Chapter 8

Family Ties

Both '96

All through supper Chris kept looking at Kat, every once in a while shaking his head and smiling. I knew what he was thinking about and it made me feel good to know that after the original shock had worn off and he'd had time to think about it, he was happy about being Kat's father.

By the time supper was over it was time for Kat to take a bath, brush her teeth and get ready for bed. As she ran up to get her pajamas head for the bathroom and wait for me to help her with her bath, I asked Chris if he'd like to read her a story and help me tuck her in. His face lit up like a Christmas tree. After she brushed her teeth and hopped in bed, I asked her if it was alright if Chris read her the story tonight. She smiled shyly and said if he wanted to, it was okay with her. I don't know which one of them enjoyed it more. By the time Chris had finished the story, they'd spent as much time laughing and giggling, if not more, as Chris had reading. She finally fell asleep clutching a teddy bear that Kari had given her earlier in the day.

As we walked out of the room, Chris said, "I still find it hard to believe that I've actually got another child," He shook his head and smiled, then continued, "She's adorable."

"I know," laughing as I said it.

"What are you laughing about woman?" He asked with a grin.

"You two. I wonder how much of that story either one of you will actually remember, you were both so busy laughing I'm surprised you got it finished at all. And giggling?? I didn't know you were a giggler, Chris" I prodded him jokingly in the ribs.

"Only when it comes to cute little girls with big brown eyes," he said as he rubbed his ribs, acting like I had actually hurt him, trying make me feel bad, "Another daughter," he said again, more to himself than to me. "She's got my eyes, huh?" His face was filled with a sense of wonder.

"Yeah, that's what I've always thought too. I've always told her she had her fathers eyes, my hair and her own personality. The first time I told her that she asked me what a pisso…nal…lity was." We laughed so hard at her question that our sides ached.

Before going to bed I looked in on my older children and told each of them that Chris and I were going to tell Kat that he was her father tomorrow. They were all excited and happy for her. Chloe and Jake said they really liked Chris and knew Kat did too, they told me they were both convinced she would be thrilled with the fact he was her father. Joe said he was glad she was finally going to get to know her dad; yawning as he said it. I kissed his forehead, (which was something I could only get away with when he was almost asleep, because he was 'at that age'), then turned off the light as I was leaving and went to take a shower.

On my way to bed I stopped off in the kitchen to make myself a cup of hot tea. When I got there I saw Chris was at the stove, "I was about to make myself a cup of hot tea. Would you like one?"

Laughing, I said, "Great minds really *do* think alike, don't they. That's just what I came in here to do." I went to the cabinet and got two cups.

Chris poured hot water over the tea bags I'd put in our cups, added sugar to his and pushed the sugar bowl across the table to me. I put some in my tea and began stirring, "Couldn't sleep, huh?" I said as I laid my spoon on the napkin beside the cup.

"Too many thoughts running through my head. I wish you *would* have told me about Kat years ago, but at least I know now. Thank you for giving me the chance to be in on the rest of her life."

"I'm glad she'll have you there for her," he reached across the table and held my fingers in his hand, "It will be good for her." I gently squeezed his fingers with mine.

He held my hand in a firm but gentle grip as he told me, "I think it will be good for both of us, *all* of us for that matter."

"I'm sure it will. She's a lot like you, she has so many of your mannerisms. She's got that habit you've always had of tossing your head to get the hair out of your eyes instead of just using your hand to push it back. She's done it since she first got hair, which wasn't until she was almost two years old, then it seemed like almost overnight she suddenly had a head full of it."

"My mom told me I didn't really have much hair either, until I was almost two years old. And those dimples, those she ***Definitely*** got from me!" He said with a grin, causing the crease he had on each cheek to deepen into dimples. I reached across the table and traced one of them with my index finger. "God Em, the things you do to me," he said breathlessly.

Kim broke the spell as she walked into the kitchen, "I couldn't sleep so I thought I'd have a cup of hot tea." Chris and I started laughing and she looked at us like we'd lost our minds. By the time I finished my tea I was yawning.

Chris saw me trying to cover my mouth with my hand as I yawned, "Maybe you should think about getting some sleep Em. We have a lot to do tomorrow."

"I think you're right, Chris, I am tired." I rose from my chair and carried my cup to the sink, rinsed it out and headed for the doorway. As I passed the table I stopped, bent down and kissed the top of Chris' head.

"Good night Chris, I'll see you in the morning. Good night Kim. Sweet dreams." Then I made my way to bed.

Laying in bed I began thinking about tomorrow and how Kat would feel when she learned that Chris was her father. I knew she liked him, I could tell by the way she had acted when he read her the story earlier.

My last thought before falling asleep was about what Chris had said to me at the table when I'd reached out to trace the dimple on his cheek with my finger. I went to sleep smiling.

Chapter 9

Mt. Pleasant

Em '76

It was hard to say good bye to the kids in the neighborhood that we'd grown so close to since moving here at the end of February, but the thought of having a place to live where we could actually turn around without bumping into each other helped ease the pain. So did the thought of each of us having our own room with a *REAL BED* in it; we had all been waking up with a sore back from sleeping on the hard, uncomfortable beds in the camper so we were more than ready for real beds.

Mom called grandma in Kansas and asked her if she would mind hiring some people to rent a U-Haul and have them bring our stuff to us. Grandma said she was way ahead of her and had already lined up some guys to do just that and our stuff would be here sometime in the evening two days from now. Mom told us the news and said it would be nice to be able to cook in a real kitchen again. Then she muttered another one of her old sayings, one about too many cooks spoiling the soup, or broth, or something like that.

Three days later we had said all the farewells we could handle, and at seven in the morning we all climbed into our vehicles. Karli went with Dad in the U-Haul, Mom and Jaicie were in the 'vette and Ren and I took the truck. After a half hour of driving we reached Mt. Pleasant, a nice enough little town, for as small as it was. Dad pulled into the parking lot of the Mt. Pleasant General Store and Mom and Rennie pulled in beside him, we all went in to check it out Inside the small store it was easy to imagine having slipped back in time to the days of penny candy and soda fountains; dozens of different, multi colored candies sat in glass containers along the counter top. The scents of cinnamon, vanilla, peppermint and root beer barrels filled the air. Behind the counter stood an old man who looked to be older than Methuselah. Dad bought us each a soda and a candy bar, picking up a sack full of the colorful candies for Karli. Mom picked up a little food and some cleaning supplies she knew we would need, then dad paid the old man at the counter and we went out to get back in the vehicles to drive the rest of the way to Bailey's Pond, and our new home.

As Rennie and I were getting ready to pull out of the parking lot we saw a blue truck pulling in. We couldn't keep ourselves from staring at the two guys who got out of it. They were gorgeous!!! I looked at Rennie and saw she was looking at me and we were *both* smiling. We both turned our heads back at the same time to look at them again.

"Oh my God, they're walking this way!!! I can't believe it!!" I said breathlessly.

"I wonder what they want?"

"Who cares, as long as we get to meet them. They are gorgeous!!"

"Yeah, you're right. It doesn't matter what they want, just as long as we get to meet them." Our windows were down and each of them walked up to a different window. The one I thought was the best looking was actually coming to MY window. 'Oh God! I'm dreaming, I know I am! I have to be, this can't really be happening! Please, don't anybody wake me up if I'm dreaming.' I thought to myself as I turned toward the window and came face to face with him.

"Hi, I'm Chris, Chris Dixon. You must be part of the family that's renting Ray's grandparents old farmhouse out at the pond." He said, as he grinned, showing the most perfect dimples I'd ever seen. I had to force myself to keep from reaching out and tracing one of them with my finger. "It's nice to finally get to meet you and I'm sure we'll see each other around a lot because Ray and I both work part-time for his grandparents at the sawmill, which isn't too far from the house your family rented. We didn't expect you to get here so early in the morning."

"That will be nice. I hope we do. My name is Em and this is my sister Rennie," I said, in a voice that squeaked, sounding more like Karli's than mine, pointing toward Ren. I cleared my throat, which helped to clear my head and continued, "we call her Ren. We didn't expect to be here so early in the morning either, but our parents wanted to get on the road as early in the day as we could so we would be able to kinda get the house set up, before we went to bed." I could hear Rennie and the other guy talking at her window and I heard him tell her his name was Ray Bailey and it was his grandparent's farm we would be living at. I could tell by her voice she was having as hard a time talking to Ray as I was to Chris. We had never even *seen* guys that looked as good as these two did, not even on television or in magazines.

"Well, I guess we better let you go for now so you can catch up with the rest of your family. We wouldn't want you two getting lost before you even got to see your new house, **OR** before we got to see you again and can get the chance to know you better. It was nice meeting you, and like I said, I'm sure we'll see a *lot* more of each other."

Ray was saying pretty much the same thing to Ren, then he and Chris turned and started walking back toward the general store. We watched them as they walked away, both of us very much enjoying the view.

"Those were the two *best* looking guys I've ever seen in my entire life!!"

"Yeah, me too. Why didn't we have guys like that in Kansas? Did you hear the way Chris said they wanted to get to know us better?! I wonder if they're going out with anybody?" I said as Rennie pulled out of the parking lot to catch up with the rest of the family, before we got too far behind them.

"I hope not!!"

"DITTO!! I DO believe I'm gonna like it here! In fact, I think I may even grow to *love* living here, some aspects of it more than others, of course" I said as I turned around to see if I could still see Chris and Ray back at the general store. "They're still standing there Ren. I wonder if they're talking about us? Oh yeah, I *AM* going to like it here. *Especially* if they aren't going out with anybody."

"I hear ya', Em, I hear ya'!" she laughed.

We caught up with the rest of the family just as they were about to reach the turn that would take us to the road that our driveway was on. About three miles down the road Dad turned onto a long curvy gravel road that stretched for what seemed like miles but was actually only about three quarters of a mile long. As we neared the end of the driveway, there was one fork leading to the North and one heading to the South. We took the South fork, pulled up a small hill and got our first look at our new house.

It was a pretty scene. The house was set on top of a hill surrounded by trees with a large front porch and tall windows all across the front. I could hardly wait to see what the inside looked like. It seemed like we were *all* pretty eager to get inside to see what it looked like because every one of us, except Dad, jumped out of our vehicles and practically ran to the front door. We had to wait for dad to unlock it and he was taking his own sweet time, teasing us because he knew how eager we all were to get inside. Finally, he unlocked the door and we all poured into the house.

It needed a little work, but only a little and it *was* beautiful. Especially to us, due to having spent the last three months crammed into a camper that was meant for vacationing in, *not* for living in. I had to admit that living in the camper *had* brought our family closer together, in more ways than just the obvious. It would be nice though to live in a house that was actually meant for a family the size of ours, instead of a tiny camper.

Just inside the front door was the living room, a large room that ran along the entire front of the house and had windows all the way from the floor to the ceiling; through an archway we could see the dining room with another archway on the other side of it that led to a huge kitchen, which made Mom *very* happy, since she would be spending a lot of her time there because she loved to cook. To the left of the dining room was a hallway, straight ahead in it was the biggest bathroom I had ever seen, that one room was bigger than the entire camper; turning left led you to a large bedroom that would be mom and dads room; to the right of the bathroom was another bedroom that would be Karli's. The steps leading to the upstairs as well as the ones going to the downstairs were in the kitchen. Upstairs was a bedroom, the half bath and a playroom, Jace was going to get the bedroom upstairs. Downstairs were two more bedrooms, another full bath and the den.

We all helped unload the U-Haul and camper; even Karli, who really wasn't much help because, at only four years old she was constantly underfoot, but she did try. Being a *very active* child, she had been having a harder time than the rest of us being cooped up in such a small space for three months. Like all kids her age, those three months had seemed more like three **years**. She was so excited about being out of the camper that mostly she just ran around enjoying the freedom she felt at having so much room to run in.

Chapter 10

Black Heart

Chris '96

"I think I've finally reached 100% certainty on why we aren't 'infected' by this evil."

"So, do I get to know yet why we all got so lucky?"

"Yep, I'm sure now so I can say it out loud. I can't believe it's something so damn simple and I've overlooked it for so long. But, I checked all of our medical records last night; thank goodness you thought to bring yours and the kids' along in case any of you got sick while you were here, which hopefully none of you will need. There's a lot to be said for planning ahead and being prepared, huh?"

"Chris!! Just tell me what it is! I'm on pins and needles here!!"

"We're all anemic *and* we don't eat beef."

"What?!?! That's it?!? That's *all* it is?!?"

"Uh huh, I told you it was simple."

"I didn't think you meant quite *THAT SIMPLE* Chris!! Mom always drummed it into our heads that not eating beef was good for our health, what with all the preservatives and other stuff they put in it when it's processed; but I'm sure she *never*, not even in her wildest dreams, thought it would protect us from evil;" I silently thanked my mother for her concern for our health, even though when I was younger, it had driven me crazy, "and here I used to worry about the kids and I being anemic but I guess it's turned out to be a blessing in disguise, hasn't it."

"You got that right! Anyway, from what I've gathered at town meetings and from talking to some of the townspeople, the evil gets into the cattle in the area, then when the people eat the beef from those infected cattle, the evil enters their bodies. The evil then 'feeds' on the energy caused by the infected blood coursing through their bodies. It seems to only affect the cattle raised in this area though, with the cattle closest to the pond affected the most. The beef is processed locally then sold at the General Store in town. The people that get infected by it seem to *need* even more of it, which gives the evil even more control over them. The more they eat, the more they need, which in turn gives the evil more control. The bigger the need, the more control and so the cycle continues."

"That explains why the closer anyone got to Bailey's Pond the stranger they got. They were closer to the source of it all when they were near the pond."

"Right, and the more distance they put between themselves and the pond the better they acted; though as long as they continued to eat the infected beef they were never really entirely free from the evil. Beef helps to combat anemia, so our not eating it has helped us to remain anemic, and while that's normally *not* a good thing to be, in this case it has served to provide a cushion, a …. barrier of sorts between us and the evil; making it so we aren't affected as much, if at all, by the evil. Such a simple thing, right under my nose the whole time and it took me this long to figure it out completely. I suspected it before, but I couldn't be sure until I looked over the medical records you brought with you, as well as mine and my kids' medical records."

"Don't you mean right under our *skin*?" I teased. He grinned at my lame attempt at humor. But, lame or not, it did help lighten the mood somewhat. "If being anemic has helped insulate us all in some way from this evil, I'll never again complain about being worn out. And I never even want to *look* at another hamburger," I laughed.

"DITTO!! From studying all our medical records I have learned a few things that still bother me."

"Such as?"

"The main one is that Kat is the least anemic of us all so she's slightly more susceptible. Hopefully, it won't matter much and she'll still be able to keep a barrier between her and whatever it is that's out there."

"I never thought I'd hear myself asking this question about one of my own children; but is there any way we can make Kat *more* anemic?"

"I'm not sure, but I can check. I know some doctors I can e-mail, I'll ask them. One thing we can do, is to make sure that she doesn't *ever* eat any beef."

"I wonder if her being less anemic is why she's always been so much more energetic and happier than her brother's and sister and I? I never could understand where she got all that energy from, my other kids were never lethargic but they didn't even come close to matching the energy she has when they were her age; and I don't remember me *ever* having that much energy. My sister Karli was a hyperactive child and I don't think even *she* had as much energy as Kat seems to have."

"I think that's a definite possibility. My other kids never had as much energy as she does either and neither did I. That's something else I can ask the doctors when I e-mail them. By the way, there's another town meeting tonight, would you like to go with me?"

""Just try and stop me."

We told the kids we were going to the town council meeting this evening so would be having supper a little earlier than usual. Although Chris' kids knew what was going on, mine didn't and I knew it was time to let them in on everything.

"Chris, I need to tell my kids what's going on. Do you have any ideas on *how* I could tell them?"

"Sure, I'll even help you, if you want me to."

"That would be great! I don't even know where to start."

"OK, we can tell them this afternoon if you want, before we go to the town council meeting."

"Works for me. But I don't want Kat to know yet, if ever. I know she's smart enough to understand but I'm not so sure she's emotionally ready to handle anything like this. I don't know many kids her age that could handle something like this."

"I agree. CJ is at a friend's house so I'll have Kim and Kari keep her occupied while we tell the others. I'm sure the girls won't mind spending time with their little sister," He smiled.

"Good idea."

It took most of the afternoon to explain to JJ, Chloe and Joe what was going on. Chris had to answer most of their questions, as well as some of mine, because there was still quite a bit I didn't know about this.

"So, you're telling us that somebody put something …. *Evil* into a pond almost thirty years ago and it's getting ready to hatch or something like that?" Chloe asked, shivering at the thought. "And that the evil infects the cattle so when the people eat it they become infected and the more they eat, the more they need."

"That's about the size of it, hon." I answered before Chris did.

"Are we gonna get …. *Infected* …. or whatever?" Joe put in, "I don't think I'd like that very much." We laughed at his remark.

"No Joe, none of us here will be affected by it."

"Why not?" JJ wanted to know.

"Because we don't *eat* the beef that is *infected* by the evil and we're all anemic. Not eating beef helps us *remain* anemic."

"Anemic??" Joe wasn't sure what that meant.

"That means our blood doesn't have enough iron and some other stuff in it," JJ supplied, before Chris got the chance to explain it to Joe.

"*GR-R-R-O-O-OSS*!! I HATE blood!!" Chloe had always hated anything at all that had to do with blood. I always teased her about it and told her I knew she was one kid of mine that was never going to become a doctor. She always rolled her eyes at me when I teased her about it.

"Yeah Chloe, but think about it; it's because we *are* anemic that we don't have to worry about that evil they're talking about," JJ reminded her.

"Cool, I like the sound of that. So I guess there *is* something good to be said for blood after all. I guess grandma was right all those times she told us beef wasn't good for us, huh Mom." she admitted. "Mom, remind me I don't *ever* want to go to McDonalds or Wendys or anyplace even remotely like them again, will you," She shivered again, thinking about all the times she and her friends had gone out to eat at all the popular fast food restaurants, "even if I do usually only eat fries."

"My sentiments exactly." I told her. They all admitted the thought frightened them a little but they thought they could deal with it and told us if there was ever anything they could do to help, we just had to let them know. By the time we finished I had learned a little bit more about what was going on too. "Remember kids, we don't want Kat to know what's been going on around here, so we need to watch what we say when she's around."

"No problem, Mom. You know we can keep secrets from her," they all assured me.

"I know you can, I just wanted to make sure you knew she isn't to know any of this."

"Gotcha, Mom!"

As soon as we were done with the explanations we started supper. When we got done eating Chris and I went to get ready for the town council meeting. I hoped the man with black eyes would ***not*** be there. I didn't think I was quite ready to meet him yet.

Chapter 11

Family Ties

Both - '96 and '90

'96-   I woke up as I'd gone to sleep, smiling. I decided my mother had been right when she had told me that the last thought you have before falling asleep is usually what you're going to dream about. My last thought had been about Chris and I'd spent the night dreaming about our time together in Vegas in '90.

'90-   We couldn't believe it when we bumped in to each other, *literally*, as we were both running to get the same taxi. It turned out we were both in town to close deals. My agent had sent me to Vegas to meet with a publisher about my first book. Emily, my agent had wanted to come with me but at the last minute something urgent had come up and she couldn't make it. After having been assured by her that I would do fine on my own, she sent me to Vegas. Chris was there to finalize the deal on some registered horses he was buying for his farm/ranch outside Mt. Pleasant.

Our meetings happened to be in the same building so we shared the taxi. We spent the entire ride catching up on what we had each been doing since the last time we had seen each other, fourteen years ago. I told him about my marriage and children, about the death of my husband in '84 in the plane crash and about the book I'd just finished. He said he had been married too, he also had three children, his wife had died in '84 too in a car accident; and that he owned a farm/ranch between Mt. Pleasant and Guion's Ferry.

My meeting was on the top floor while his was on the fifteenth, as he got off the elevator on the fifteenth floor we made plans for dinner that night. As the elevator continued its ascent, I couldn't help but marvel at the similarities in our lives and wondered if our meeting here again after all this time was mere coincidence or if some greater force was at work. I didn't really care, whichever it was, I was just pleased to see him again.

After reading the contract the publisher, Susan Simms, had drafted, I explained to her that I would have to have my agent look it over and if she agreed to the terms we had a deal. She said that was fine and she would be waiting to hear from one of us. I thanked her, we shook hands and I left her office to return to the hotel to get ready for my dinner with Chris.

I looked over the contract again in the taxi on the way back to the hotel. While it wasn't what the famous authors brought in, it was still quite a bit for a first book by an unknown. The kids would be thrilled and I knew my agent, Emily Clark, would be just as thrilled as they were, if not more. Her estimate of what she thought the publisher would offer for a first book was quite a bit below the amount in the contract, which meant her commission was going to be a good deal more than she'd estimated. YEP, she *would* be thrilled!! I planned to fax her a copy of the contract as soon as I got back to the hotel. I smiled as I thought of the look on her face when she saw it and I wished I could be there to see it. Then I thought of dinner with Chris tonight and decided that no matter how fond I was of Emily, I would much rather be looking at Chris.

I didn't know what to wear to dinner because Chris hadn't told me where we were going or if I was supposed to dress up or not. I finally decided on a strapless, royal blue dress that I thought was a little too short, while my daughter Chloe disagreed and said the dress made me look glamorous, but not pretentious. She made sure she also told me that I didn't need the dress for that, because I looked great in whatever I wore. I smiled at the memory.

After curling my hair and piling it on top my head and putting clips in to hold it; I put on heels that matched the dress and picked up a matching handbag. Just then I heard a knock on the door to my suite. I felt butterflies fluttering around in my stomach, just the way they had the first time I had met Chris.

Opening the door, I was glad I had decided to dress up because Chris was facing me dressed in an expensive suit that was just a couple of shades darker than the dress I was wearing. 'My God, he's as gorgeous as ever,' I thought to myself as we stood and stared at each other for what seemed like hours, but was actually only a few minutes before either of us could speak. Then we both started talking at the same time.

"You haven't changed a bit Chris."

"I believe I'd rather stand here looking at you than go to dinner."

"You look the same as you did when we went to prom together fourteen years ago." When we realized we were both talking, therefore couldn't either one hear what the other was saying, we started laughing.

"You first." Chris told me.

"You haven't changed a bit since we went to prom together fourteen years ago." I finally realized I was blocking the doorway so I moved aside and said, "Would you like to come in?"

'And I was saying you look beautiful and I'd rather stand here looking at you than go to dinner. And, no, I *don't* think it would be a good idea for me to come in, because I'm afraid if I did, we might not *make* it to dinner. Maybe it would be better if we just went straight to the restaurant." He grinned and the dimples I remembered so well showed up. I reached out to trace one of them with my index finger like I used to all those years ago. "God, Em, the things you do to me!" It was the same thing he'd said every time I'd done it years ago. I stepped out of my suite and locked the door. Chris took my arm in his and led me to the bank of elevators.

Later, as we were leaving the restaurant , I told him dinner had been wonderful, "I can't believe you remembered my fondness for seafood. Especially lobster."

"There's a lot I remember about you Em, you're a hard person to forget."

So are you, believe me. It's strange isn't it, the things a person remembers."

"Such as?"

"Oh, you know what I mean, things you thought you'd forgotten suddenly pop back into your head."

"I know what you mean, I was just trying to get a rise out of you like I used to whenever I would tease you."

"I think raising children by myself took care of that for me. I've learned you can't let the little things get to you, if you do, the big things will overwhelm you."

"That's one of the things I've learned too since Alyssa died and I was thrust instantly into the role of single parent. I also learned I was glad we had only had three kids, I don't know if I could have dealt with any more than that at the time. I'd only wanted two children but Alyssa had her heart set on three, so three It was. When I first found out she was pregnant for the third time I got angry; over time though I came to realize that my anger wouldn't solve anything. By the time Kari was born we'd reached the agreement that there wouldn't be any more children. *Ever*. I love kids, don't get me wrong but I thought that with the world in the shape it was in, why keep bringing more innocent children in to it. Now I wouldn't trade any of my kids for all the money in the world. I love them more than life itself."

"I understand how you feel. I have always thought the world was not the best place to be bringing an over-abundance of children into either. We only wanted two children too, so Joe kind of came as a shock to Jake and I. I had been taking the pill since JJ and Chloe's birth two years earlier, but I guess we forgot that no form of birth control other than total abstinence is one hundred percent effective. Being married, we were not about to do the abstinence thing, so I chose the pill. NOT a good choice, let me tell you, before we knew it we were soon to be a family of five, instead of four. After the initial shock wore off though, we were happy and by the time he was born we were all looking forward to it, especially JJ and Chloe. After his birth the doctor changed my prescription so I wouldn't get pregnant again, and so far, knock on wood, I haven't."

We'd been walking as we talked and had reached the door to my suite, "Would you like to come in for a while?"

"I don't think I should, I'm not sure what would happen if I get you and a bed in the same room. How long will you be in town?"

"I was wondering what would happen too. I must admit though, at the risk of sounding…. Cheap… I was kind of hoping something *would* happen, I've missed you so much Chris," My face turning red as I said it. I hurried on, "I was planning on staying at least another night, maybe longer."

"I think you're the only woman your age that still blushes. It's cute." He reached out and stroked my cheek, "Another night at least huh? How about spending the day with me tomorrow then having dinner together again? A friend of mine told me about a little out of the way seafood place that has great food and all the shrimp you can eat. You're not he only one that loves seafood. Shrimp….. M-m-m-m." He licked his lips as he said the last part and as he did, I regretted again that he wouldn't be coming into my room tonight.

I cleared my throat, which helped to clear my head and said, "That sounds wonderful. I guess I'll see you in the morning then."

It's a date," he said as he leaned forward and kissed my lips gently, tracing them lightly with his tongue before turning to go to his own suite three doors down the hall.

It took a few minutes before I recovered from the feel of his lips once again touching mine, the feel of his tongue tracing my lips. Finally I turned to unlock the door to my suite and went in to spend the night dreaming about him.

'96-   "Mommy!! Mommy!! Guess what? Kim said I could go out on the lake today on the houseboat! She said all the kids were going!" She lunged on the bed.

"Make sure you wear your lifejacket."

"Mo-o-om!"

"Ka-a-at!" She laughed like she always did when I mocked her. "So munchkin, how do you like it here so far?"

"I L-O-V-E it, Mommy!" She was an exceptional child and was already learning to spell, so she now had a tendency to spell out words that were special to her, "there's so much to do and they're all so nice. I wish we didn't **ever** have to leave!!" As she said this she jumped off the bed to get my brush off the vanity so she could brush my hair, she had loved brushing my long hair since she first learned how. My hair had never really been cut, merely had the dead ends cut off every few months; so it reached to a point past my knees. Even when it was braided, I sometimes still sat on it, so I usually just braided it and pulled it around to the front, over my shoulder.

As I turned so she could brush, I noticed through the open doorway that Chris was standing in the hall just outside my room. By the look on his face I could tell he had heard her last remark. He smiled.

Chapter 12

Life At The Pond

Em '76

The first thing any of us wanted to do when we got inside was to set up the beds so we could sleep in a real bed for the first time in months. That done, we each carried our own stuff to our rooms, with all of us helping Karli with hers. After getting everything off the U Haul, we began putting things where they belonged. Soon we had the front room and dining room in order and had everything at least *in* the rooms the stuff belonged in. By suppertime we had accomplished quite a bit but there was still a lot to be done. At six o'clock we all sat at the table in the dining room for our first meal in our new house.

"Voila'! Our first meal in our new home!" Mom exclaimed as she set the platter of veg' burgers (as she liked to call them) on the dining room table. It may not have been anything fancy but to us it seemed like a seven course meal; of course we *had* been working all day and were starving. But Mom really was a great cook, she always had been.

Except for last year, when the only other choice had been to starve, our family had never been much for eating meat. Mom didn't like the idea of all those preservatives going in our bodies, she said it wasn't good for us to have so many things in our bodies that didn't belong there. So, while we did eat *some* pork, lamb once in a while and a *lot* of fish and seafood, we mostly ate a lot of what wee liked to call 'rabbit food'; green stuff, fruits, vegetables, whole grain foods. Things that were 'good for us', as Mom liked to say. 'You are what you eat' was another on of her favorite old sayings; and she managed to come up with at least one of them a day.

"Just think Ren, tonight we won't have to clean off the table so we can make our bed out of it," I noticed the look Mom gave me, "We'll still have to clean it off, but at least it *won't* be because we need it to make our bed with." Mom smiled.

"That'll be nice, huh," Ren said, reaching for another burger. "For the first time in a long time I'm actually looking forward to going to bed." We all wholeheartedly agreed with her comment.

"I just hope I can sleep with all the quiet around here," Jace worried, "I've never heard so much quiet. It's eerie."

"How can you *hear* quiet, Jace?" Karli wanted to know.

"It's just a figure of speech, kiddo," Dad explained, patting her on top the head.

"Oh, one of tho-ose!" she said , acting like she knew exactly what he meant although we all knew she wasn't quite sure. She did that a lot; acting like she knew more than she really did, but it was cute and she was actually pretty smart, for a kid her age.

"Dinner was great hon," Dad said as he got up from the table, "I think I'll go try to get the den in some kind of order. It looks like hurricane Karli went through it." He grinned at the joke. Karli did seem to be able to mess up a lot for someone her size. "If you need me, that's where I'll be. Don't forget we need to talk to Karli about staying away from the pond unless she has one of the rest of us with her."

"I'll remember, believe me." Mom was terrified of the water. She had been since, as a child, she had almost drowned. She would make sure that anytime Karli, (or Jace either, for that matter), even got *near* the water they would have their lifejackets on and Dad knew it. He was only mentioning it because he wanted Mom to remind him about it in case he got too busy and forgot, which he sometimes tended to do. "After you girls clean off the table and get the dishwasher started you can go down and check out the pond if you want to."

"COOL!" I could hardly wait to see the pond that had given our new home it's name.

"Be careful though, you know how I feel about water."

Ren and I hurried to finish our chores so we could get down to the pond. Jace wanted to put up her posters and finish arranging her room and Karli wanted to 'help' Dad in the study, (as if! We were sure he would be just thrilled at having her help), so Ren and I were the only ones going to the pond.

"How long do you think it will be before we see those two guys again, Ren?" I asked as we reached the bottom of the small hill, then turned to go up the North fork of the road. It was hard to believe it could be so quiet.

"I don't know, but I hope it's not too long. I think Ray liked me and Chris was sure staring at you this morning," she teased.

"No more than I was staring at him. God, he was cute!!" We laughed at ourselves.

Just ahead was a small curve in the road, as we went around it to the East we got our first look at Bailey's Pond. "Its beautiful!" I said, quietly, as if I didn't want to disturb the beauty.

"It sure is," Ren agreed, speaking just as quietly as I had.

Across the pond was a high rock cliff that looked to be dotted with cliffs. "It looks so peaceful." (Little did we know of the terrors lurking beneath the serene beauty; waiting, hiding, incubating, wanting to be born but not yet quite ready to make it's entrance into the world. It would be years before the full scope of the evil hidden in it's depths would be realized.)

A small rowboat was pulled to the shore closest to where we were standing. Ren and I decided to row across the pond to see if the dots we'd seen from the West side of the lake were caves or not. We tied the boat to a small bush and looked up the face of the cliff, it *was* full of small caves. We decided against entering any of them until our dad was there because he really enjoyed exploring caves; or spelunking, as he called it, which is what it was actually called, but exploring was easier to say. Our dad liked using the technical names for everything, he said it helped teach us the correct terms for things, and he **always** liked being correct.

The cliff had steps carved along it that would make it easy for us to reach the top so we climbed to the top of the high cliff. We couldn't tell if the steps were man-made or had been made by nature. From the top of the cliff we could see all the way around the pond, it was a beautiful sight. To the North we could see that the road we'd come in on went all the way around the pond and continued off to the East somewhere. The Southside was a large, flat, green meadow that would be perfect for family picnics or sunbathing, or as someplace to just get away from everyone in case you ever wanted to be alone. Off to the Southwest we could see our house, the camper and vehicles parked in front of it and the pumphouse for our well. Farther off in that direction we could just make out the top of the Bailey sawmill. Looking around, I decided it was the most beautiful spot I'd ever seen.

After watching the sun set behind the trees, "We'd better head back before Mom sends out a search party, you know how much she worries." Ren said as she started back down the cliff to the boat. Reluctantly, I followed. We rowed slowly back to the spot we'd found the small rowboat, pulled it up on the shore and headed for the house.

It had been a long day, so after telling Mom about the two cute guys we'd met outside the general store that morning, and the conversation we had with them; and asking Dad when he thought we could all go exploring in the caves, (except Mom, she didn't like doing things like that. Dad had always joked with her about it and called her his 'Nature Girl') we said goodnight to them. Rennie and I had gotten the downstairs bedrooms so we headed downstairs together. Saying goodnight to each other, we headed to our rooms. The bed felt so good after having slept in the camper for so long that I think I was asleep before my head hit the pillow.

I woke the next morning to the sound of birds waking up; somebody's dog barking at the cattle in the field to the South of us and the soft, distant rumble of the sawmill starting it's work for the day. I lay in bed for a while, enjoying the solitude, as well as the comfort of the bed, then rose to get ready for another day of getting the house in order. By the time I reached the kitchen and got the coffee going for Mom and Dad, the rest of the family began straggling in.

After breakfast was over and the dishwasher was loaded, Mom said she had a big surprise for us, "Since you girls worked so hard yesterday to help get everything unloaded, unpacked and *mostly* arranged I've decided that today we're all going to take some time off." This *was* a big surprise, as she usually made a point of letting us know that 'there's a place for everything, and everything in it's place'; which was her old saying for letting us know we needed to do some housekeeping. Looking around, I could see that everything definitely **wasn't** in it's place. But, as she was so fond of saying, 'never look a gift horse in the mouth' so I was definitely *not* going to point out everything that still needed to be done. Her voice broke into my thoughts, "So, go do whatever you want, but be careful."

She asked Ren and I if we would mind making a run into town for her to pick up some more food and cleaning supplies. We had no problem with that, especially because it meant we might get to see Chris and Ray in town again.

When we got to town we drove around to see where things were, which didn't take long because it was a *very* small town. It consisted of the general store, a post office directly across the highway from that, a second hand store next to the post office, a school and about forty five to fifty five houses. The school was on a hill behind the general store, the driveway leading in to it was off the road to the East of the general store, the road continuing on past the school to the North then curving West. We found out later that week that the road continued West to become the road that ran along the North side of Bailey's Pond. We also found out that it was a shortcut to town (as long as it wasn't raining or hadn't rained for a few days, in which case it was a muddy mess) and that Ray's family lived on that road at the Northwest edge of Mt. Pleasant.

We were sorry we didn't see Chris or Ray in town that morning but we knew in a place this small it wouldn't be long before we would see them again. We picked up the stuff Mom wanted from the general store and started for home. When we reached our long driveway, we both saw the truck coming from the direction of our house at the same time. It was the same truck we'd seen the day before at the general store, Chris and Ray had been at our house while we'd been in town! They pulled up to the stop sign at the end of the driveway just as we pulled in.

"Hi, we've been looking for you," Ray said as we pulled up beside them.

"Yeah, we wanted to know if you wanted to go to the fair in Calico Rock with us. It starts tomorrow. We asked your mom already and she said it was fine with her but shouldn't we be asking you."

"You actually asked our mother if we could go out with you?!" I said incredulously. Nobody had *ever* asked our parents if they could go out with us before.

""Why, is that a no-no?" Chris asked, grinning.

"No, it's just that nobody has ever asked either of our parents for permission to go out with us before. I bet Mom loved it, she's always telling us that 'most kids these days just don't have enough respect for their elders,' we laughed at my perfect imitation of Mom's voice. "She'll probably be thrilled that we've finally met some polite, respectful boys. At least that's how she'll put it."

"That's us, polite Chris and respectful Ray," Ray laughed as he said it, "Seriously though, do you think you might want to go with us? It should be a lot of fun."

"Sure," Ren and I said at the same time.

"We'll be here tomorrow at noon to pick you up then. OK?"

"We'll be ready," I told them, "See you tomorrow." We watched as they drove off toward town. "God Ren, they actually asked us out!"

""What are we gonna wear? What will we do with our hair? I hope we have enough makeup and stuff." She said aloud.

When we reached the house Mom told us she'd met them and had been very impressed by their polite, respectful behavior, (which was exactly what I had said she'd say, Ren and I grinned and poked each other in the sides knowingly). As we were heading downstairs to decide what we were going to wear on our date the next day we heard Mom from the top of the stairs, "I can see why you like them, they *are cute*, aren't they. You guys all have fun tomorrow." She smiled as she turned around and headed for the kitchen to begin fixing supper.

"Oh yeah!!" We said in unison, "Cute is one thing they *definitely* are!" We spent the next two hours deciding what to wear and how we were going to fix our hair. We both had long thick hair that hung to our waists, Ren's black and mine dark blonde.

We had a lot of fun at the fair the next day with the guys and got home around midnight. Mom was waiting up for us and we told her all about it. We told her it had been a lot of fun and that Chris and Ray had asked us if maybe we would think about going steady with them. We told her that of course we had said yes, she laughed and said she could certainly understand why we had both said yes. After that night, we were all inseparable. So much so, that people began calling us the 'Four Musketeers'. The only time we were separated was when we had to go home at night and we didn't like having to be apart from each other even then. It was the best summer of my life.

Chapter 13

Town Meeting

Both '96

"Remember Em, they don't know that some people are immune to their masters evil. I didn't want to tip them off, so whenever I go into town I act like I'm infected by it too." Chris told me as we drove to town for the council meeting, "Although some people may remember you from before, some of them won't know you and may be suspicious of you. I think if you just do what I've been doing, *act* like you are infected and if anyone asks, tell them you felt 'drawn back' here by some kind of force you can't explain, it should help put any suspicions any of them might have to rest. At least I hope it will. These people can be pretty dangerous."

"Will do, boss!" I said, giving him a mock salute.

His cheeks dimpled as he said "And none of that at the meeting. Believe me Em, these people are anything but fun. None of them seem to have much of a sense of humor anymore. They haven't had since that night the black eyed man came to town twenty five years ago."

"Don't worry, I'll behave myself Chris," I told him, "I can be a hell of an actress when I need to be. I guess my vivid imagination helps me a lot in that regard."

"Good, you'll need all the acting skills you have for this."

As we pulled into the parking lot of the high school I saw what must have been every vehicle in the county already there, "My God, I didn't realize it was so widespread! It looks like half the state is here."

"Yeah, it seems to be spreading faster now that the 'master' is getting ready to be born. Every meeting has more people at it than the one before. It's hard to believe from looking at the town that this many people live around here, but most of them are from the outlying countryside." He pulled in to a parking space and we got out of the truck and headed for the auditorium.

"I remember the last time we were here together. Prom night, 1977. Remember Chris?"

""I've never forgotten Em," he said as he took my hand in his, "OK, better turn on those acting skills now," as we entered the building.

I looked around and saw a few people I remembered from when I'd lived here before, a few I thought maybe I should know but couldn't quite place and quite a few people I had never set eyes on. To my left I saw the principal of the high school, Mr. Mobley talking to Mr. Graves, my old biology teacher, who I had never much cared for; off to the left I saw the longtime postmistress Mrs. Harris talking to Mr. Hillman, who was the janitor for the schools.

We took seats in the back row of chairs they had set up specifically for the meeting. People talked among themselves until the council chairman banged a gavel to call the meeting to order. Although I had been to a couple of them in my life, I had never really been one to go to town meetings much because I didn't feel they had too much of an impact on my life or the lives of those I cared about. I found out that in Mt. Pleasant whether or not you went to the town meetings could mean the difference between life and death. If someone wasn't going to be at a meeting, they had better have a damn good reason.

The council chairman, Mr. Graves, no less, banged his gavel again and the meeting began; "I'm pleased to see so many familiar faces here this evening, as well as a few new ones," his eyes traveled around the room, pausing occasionally to rest on a face here or there that he didn't recognize, mine included. However, as he began to look away from me, his head turned back and I could tell he thought maybe he should know me from somewhere. After staring at each other for a few minutes, I was relieved to see his gaze continue on around the room, searching out others he didn't know. When he was finished, he asked, "Any new business?"

Another council member, a woman who used to be, and I later found out, still was, the literature teacher said, "I noticed that some of the new people I've seen around town aren't here, also a couple that decided to move back after being away for quite a few years, the Abbott's." I seemed to recall that name from somewhere but couldn't quite figure it out before she continued, "I move we appoint some people to find out why."

"I second the motion," someone from the audience raised their hand. Throughout the course of the meeting, anything that needed seconded was done so by the same voice.

"All in favor, say aye," A loud chorus of 'ayes' echoed in the room, "All opposed, say nay," not a single voice was heard throughout the entire room, "Motion carried." He began pointing to different people around the room, "Jim, Keith, Marjorie, Chris," he pointed to Chris sitting beside me and I heard Chris sigh, as if with relief, (I made a mental note to myself to ask him on the way home why he did that) "And …" he looked across the room, finally finding the person he was looking for, "… and Helen. I nominate you five to check it out."

"I second the nomination," the voice said again.

"All in favor?" again, a chorus of ayes could be heard, "All opposed?" again, not a single voice was heard. "Motion carried. Any more new business?" No response. "OK, no more new business. Any old business?" A hand shot up in the audience, "Yes Frank?"

"I just wanted to give ya'all an update on Alice's condition," as he spoke, I realized he was the man who had run the general store for as long as anyone could remember. I knew Alice was his wife's name, "She came home from the hospital today, the doctors said they were amazed at the progress she's made so far, they've never seen someone her age heal as fast as she has. Said she was gonna be as good as new in no time at all. Thought ya'all might be happy to hear it. I know I am." The relief he felt at her speedy recovery was plain, "She also wanted to thank ya'all for keeping her in your thoughts. She wanted to come and thank you in person, but the doctors told her she had to stay in bed; for the first few days at least. After the first few days they told her she can slowly get back to business as usual. She has appointments every week for the next six weeks, then it goes down to one appointment a month for the rest of her life. That's all I had to say." He sat down.

"That's great news Frank, we're happy to hear she is doing so well," yet another member of the council, a Mrs. Frazier, spoke, "Tell her we will continue to keep her in our thoughts, if you will," he curtly nodded his agreement, "Mr. Chairman," she continued as she turned toward Mr. Graves,

"I would like to request that any newcomers we have here tonight come up front and tell us a little about themselves."

"I second that," again, from the same voice.

"No need for a second Sam;" I barely managed to stifle a laugh as I came up with a name for the man, Seconding Sam, "that wasn't a motion, simply a request," Mr. Graves told him. "No problem, Beth, we'll take care of it right now. I believe I noticed six new faces in the room tonight," glancing about the room, he pointed at the six people, of which I was one and asked us to all come to the front of the room so we could introduce ourselves to everyone and tell the assembly a little about ourselves. I groaned silently and slowly made my way to the front of the room to join the other five people in line. 'I really don't want to be up here,' I thought to myself as the first person in the short line began introducing himself.

Mr. Graves pointed to the person closest in line to him, which meant I would be the fifth one to introduce myself to the room full of people. By the time it was my turn we had met Josh Evans, a veterinarian who had just moved here from Little Rock hoping to set up a small practice around here, he was single and had no children; Jim and Danyel Miller, newlyweds who were in the area to visit her aunt, Jackie Burns, who ran the second hand store by the post office; and Walter O'Rourke, a construction worker, who told everyone his wife Sally was home with their new baby girl, who wasn't feeling well, he figured it was probably croup or something.

My turn now; I told them my name, that I was an author, my children and I were visiting my old friend Chris Dixon and his children, and that my family and I had lived at Bailey's Pond for a little over a year almost twenty years ago. A murmur of muted voices went through the room, causing Mr. Graves to bang his gavel to restore quiet. When the voices had finally subsided we met the last person in the line; Ruby Douglass, she told us she had just finished college, was about to begin a new job in Calico Rock and that she had settled in Mt. Pleasant because it seemed like a nice little town and she could afford the rent on the little house she had rented just outside town.

Not long after the introductions, with no business pending, Mr. Graves adjourned the meeting with, "May he watch over us all, in this, our time of triumph."

Some of the people left immediately following the meeting but many remained to visit with friends and relatives they didn't often get to see due to full schedules or farming duties. Chris and I stayed to see what we could find out about the pending birth of the 'master'. He said he needed to talk to the other people Graves had chosen for the committee. He walked toward a small group of people gathered in a corner of the room.

I felt a hand on my shoulder as I walked over to the refreshment table for some punch. Turning, I found myself looking into the face of Mr. Graves.

"I thought I recognized you earlier as you walked in. You were the girl that convinced most of my biology class to walk out when I said we might be dissecting a human fetus." He moved toward the cups that held the punch. "That was the 76-77 school year if I remember correctly," as he picked up a cup.

"It seemed like a good idea at the time," I said, almost in defense of my actions twenty years ago. "I hope you aren't holding it against me after all this time."

"Oh, not at all. I just wanted to let you know I remembered you and the impact you had on that class. Quite the leader, weren't you? Do you still have the power to cause such intense emotion and upheaval in large groups of people?"

"Thank you, I've always fancied myself as more of a leader than a follower. Yes, I have been told from time to time that some of my books have made quite a few people have second thoughts about their lives and want to change."

"You're very welcome. How long have you been at the Dixon's?"

"A couple of days now."

"And how long will you be staying in the area?" He asked, trying to act like he wasn't prying, which is exactly what he *was* doing.

"We're not sure yet," I decided to try what Chris had suggested; I baited the hook, "We may stay for quite a while, in fact we may never leave. There seems to be *something*, a force of some kind, that drew me back here. I can sometimes feel it trying to convince me to stay. Chris said he's felt the same way since childhood, that no matter where he went, something always pulled him back here. It is beautiful around here and my children seem to like it as much as I do."

He smiled, "Yes it does seem to have that effect on certain people, and while I've never heard of it pulling someone back after twenty years, it is entirely possible. You must care for Chris **very** deeply for it to have that effect on you after all this time. Or, there *may* be another reason why."

"I care more than anyone could know." I said, almost under my breath. "What other reason could there be that would draw me back after twenty years?"

"Oh, I know much more than people think," the way he said it, I began to wonder just *who* was baiting *whom*. "For instance, I know you and Chris ran into each other in Las Vegas in 1990." I had to work very hard to control my emotions so the shock I felt at his words wouldn't show on my face. Apparently I succeeded, because he said it was nice to have another member in the community, then said "One can never know *all* the things that are happening in the world around them, can they?" His cryptic tone of voice was beginning to really scare me, which I'm sure was exactly what he intended it to do.

"Em," I heard Chris say from behind me, "It's getting late, we better be going." It wasn't even eight o'clock yet!

"Sure Chris, I didn't realize it was getting to be so late." I played along with Chris, knowing he must have a very good reason for wanting us to leave so early. I turned to Mr. Graves, "It's been a pleasure seeing you again," I lied, "I hope we can chat again soon."

"Yes, it was good to see you again also. I'm sure we'll see each other again, soon." He turned, walking toward the small group of people Chris had just left.

Chris took my arm in his and led me out to the truck, "Why did you sigh like that when Graves picked you to be on his little 'committee'? And what was that about it getting late? It's not even eight yet. Did something happen while you were talking to that bunch of committee members that made you in such a hurry to get out of there?" Just before we reached the truck, "Chris, Graves somehow knew we had seen each other in Vegas in '90, I don't know how he knew, but he did. It scared me when he said that he knew. He made it sound like he had actually been there. I was wondering why the man with black eyes wasn't at tonight's meeting, weren't you, Chris. Doesn't he usually show up at all of them? I mean, I'm kind of glad he wasn't here tonight, because I don't know if I'm ready to meet him yet; but I do think it is kind of strange that the only town meeting I go to, he isn't at," I shivered, then wondered aloud why Graves had said what he did about people never knowing exactly what was going on in the world around them.

We got in the truck before Chris spoke, "Yes, I was wondering the same thing; he usually *is* at all the meetings, this is the first one I can remember him *not* being at since that first meeting he attended. I just hope like hell that his not being there doesn't mean that whatever that man put in that damn pond is hatching at this precise moment, and he didn't feel it was safe to leave it alone while it does." I saw the look of concern on his face. "I don't know how Graves knew we saw each other in Vegas; hell, I'm not even sure I *want* to know how he knows; he's one strange guy." I found myself silently agreeing with Chris, Graves was a really weird man. "The reason I wanted Graves to put me on his committee was because if I'm on it then maybe that will give us the chance to save at least a few innocent, uninfected people from the others on the committee."

"Save them? Save them from what Chris?"

"From being killed Em!! People in the area who don't attend the local town meetings are checked out, thoroughly, and if their reasons aren't to the satisfaction of *all* of the council members, they're terminated."

"Terminated?? But why? And why didn't you tell me this part earlier? That's a pretty big part of it Chris."

"Because if they aren't one of the 'chosen' as the council members call those who are affected, then they're outsiders and outsiders may wish to harm the 'master'." He reached out to place his hand on my arm, "You see now, why I wanted you to act like you were one of the 'chosen'? I don't want to lose you again Em, and this time it wouldn't be for twenty years, it would be permanent!" He dropped his hand from my arm, "I didn't tell you because it hasn't happened in so long; since I was a child actually, about three years after the man with black eyes showed up the first time. I didn't realize anyone besides the Abbott's had moved here lately and I was planning to go see them tomorrow. The reason I didn't realize anyone else had moved here is because I try to avoid hanging out in town as much as possible. The people there give me the creeps, Em; with the black eyed man and Graves at the top of the weird list. While you were talking to Graves, I was told who all the new people are and where they live. That's why I wanted to leave so early."

"Where are we going now?"

"We need to get to any newcomers before the rest of the committee members do and find out if they are infected or not. If they aren't, then we need to either recruit them or get them the hell out of here!"

We pulled out of the parking lot and headed for the homes of what could possibly be yet *more* innocent, unsuspecting victims of the evil that was taking over the area.

Chapter 14

Bonding

Both - '96

By the time Kat finished brushing my hair, I knew I didn't have time for even a quick shower if Chris and I were to tell her before the kids went out on the lake on the houseboat. Since I'd taken one last night though, it wouldn't really matter if I put it off for a few more hours.

I dressed quickly then Kat and I went downstairs to find Chris. We found him sitting in the glider on the back patio. I sat down beside him and pulled Kat up on to my lap, "Honey, Mommy's got something to tell you and I want to get done with as few interruptions as possible. So try not to talk unless you're asked something, OK?"

"Am I in trouble, Mommy?" She asked innocently.

I hugged her, "No sweetie, you're not in trouble," I pulled back from her and teased her, "Why? Did you do something you should be in trouble for?"

She laughed and said, "I dunno!!" It was a joke we'd played together for years. I hugged her to me then pulled back far enough I could look into her eyes.

"In that case, I'll get started." I thought about how to put it and finally began, "You remember, don't you, all the conversations we've had in the past about the other kids' dad and how you always got sad because you never got to meet your own daddy?"

"Uh-huh."

"And you remember everything I've told you about your daddy, right?"

"Yeah, you told me that I have his eyes," she giggled as she always did when she thought about that. She always wanted to know how he could see if *she* had his eyes, "his smile, a lot of his actions and the same habit he has of tossing my head to get the hair out of my eyes instead of just using my hand to push it back, and that his name is Chris," As she said the name she looked over at Chris then back to me; I could see the question in her eyes. She looked at Chris again then slowly turned to look at me again, "Mommy???" For the first time I could remember, she couldn't ask the question she'd been asking me for years, 'Is he my daddy?' Although she didn't say it out loud, the question was in her eyes. Finally, I could answer the question for her, "Yes Kat, he is."

"*Cool*!!" She jumped from my lap, hugged Chris, smothering him with kisses, then ran off yelling for her brother's and sister, "I found him!! I found my daddy! Finally!! I finally found my daddy!!!" She stopped suddenly, "That means I also got more sisters and another brother too. This is **SO WAY COOL**!!!" She took off running across the yard again, yelling for *all* of her brothers and sisters.

"Thank God you told Kim, Chris and Kari last night because they're sure enough going to know they have a little sister now." Laughing, I looked back over at Chris. He was smiling, with tears in his eyes. I reached for him just as he was reaching out for me.

"See Chris, I told you she would be happy! She's happier than I've ever seen her. She's waited so long for this moment. I'm so glad for her, and you."

"Thank you Em, for giving me such a beautiful, precious gift as her. I was kind of worried last night about how she would react when she found out but I can see now I had nothing to be worried about."

"Piece of cake!" I snapped my fingers and hugged him even tighter. I could feel the tension that had been building in him since last night ebbing out of his body as we embraced tightly. "I'm so glad her knowing made you both so happy. I knew she'd love you, I mean, come on, what's NOT to love, right. You're a lovable guy and a great dad. Thank you for giving me that beautiful, precious gift." I felt the last of the tension leave his body as I said it.

He grinned, "SO WAY COOL??"

"Sometimes she watches *way* too much television," I managed to say, before I started laughing, he began laughing with me. We were still laughing when all the kids came up to the patio; Kat wearing her lifejacket, holding Kim and Chloe's hands. "My brothers and sisters and me are going out on the houseboat now," she proudly told us. The rest of the kids were smiling at her.

"OK, just be careful."

"Be back in time for dinner," Chris said as he checked the hooks on the lifejacket to make sure they were secure, which I had just been going to do.

Letting go of her sisters' hands, Kat hugged him, then came over to me, "Thank you **so** much Mommy, I L-O-V-E him!!" She whispered loudly, in my ear as she hugged me, before running to join her brothers and sisters. Chris smiled as he heard what she had been whispering.

Since the kids were going to be out of the house for at least a few hours I decided that instead of taking a shower I was going to take a nice long bath. "I think I'll take a nice hot, relaxing bath while they're gone."

"Need any help?" Chris asked, leering at me.

"Well, I guess maybe you *could* wash my back, if you'd like," I said as I turned to go inside, like being a feeble word to describe how much I wanted him to join me in the bathtub; anticipation, desire even, but like couldn't even come close to describing my need.

He was right behind me, "I thought you'd *never* ask. You can use the master bath if you'd like, the tub is so much bigger," he offered, suggestively. We headed for the large bathroom just off the master bedroom.

"I was waiting for you to bring the subject up," I told him as I began running the bath water into the large oval tub.

"Well now, aren't we just the blind leading the blind." We laughed at his comment because it was true. Although we both wanted the same thing, neither of us wanted to appear eager to mention it. My body had yearned to feel his touch again since that last night in Vegas, almost six years ago.

Washing my back wasn't all Chris had planned to do; joining me in the tub, he not only washed my back, he made sure *all* of me was clean, I got cleaner than I had ever been in my life, and I did the same for him. Not that it really made too much of a difference because when we got out of the tub and had dried each other off, we made our way to the king sized bed that dominated his room. Our towels dropped from our bodies just before we lay down on the big bed.

"I've wanted to do this since you arrived," he said as he leaned over to touch his lips to mine.

It was so comforting to be held in his embrace after so long away, the sensation of again feeling his beating heart beneath my cheek, that I clung to him, like moss to a stone. My arms made their way up to encircle his neck and I pulled him closer to me, eagerly kissing him in return, enjoying the feel of his lips once again on mine after having been away for so long. "So have I Chris. I've wanted you since I first saw you again on the porch that first day we arrived," I agreed with him when our lips finally parted. "But I was afraid you'd be so angry about Kat, or at least that I hadn't told you about her that you wouldn't want me near you. I'm glad I was wrong."

"I could never be mad at you Em, at least not for very long. You should know that by now." He began kissing my neck; I felt my body quiver as I felt his lips touching my earlobe. "Especially about someone as adorable as Kat," he said just before he began trailing kisses from my neck down the rest of my body. There wasn't much chance for conversation after he started doing that because I was unable to speak and he was too busy. Every once in a while one of us would involuntarily mutter something or other about how good it felt to finally be together again; mostly however, we simply enjoyed the feeling of being in each others arms again, knowing the other was feeling the same pleasure.

By the time Chris had covered almost every inch of my body with his kisses I had begun kissing his body. Starting with his fingertips, I worked my way up his arm, then to the rest of him. I don't know which of us was enjoying it more. I enjoyed touching him and he enjoyed being touched; he enjoyed touching me and I definitely enjoyed being touched by him.

An hour and a half later, we lay back on the bed, satisfied, for now. "God, I'd forgotten how much fun that is!"

"Yeah, it's been a long time for me too," I said as I reached over to the night stand to get the cigarettes and lighter. I lit two and after passing him one, I continued, "Almost six years as a matter of fact."

"Me too. After our time in Vegas, nobody else seemed to interest me," he glanced over at me and grinned, "And don't you go getting the idea that you ruined me for all other women," he teased.

"'MOI!' Perish the thought!" Laughing, we finished our cigarettes, "I guess we should be getting dressed. The kids will be back soon."

"We should be getting downstairs," he said at the same time. Laughing again, "There go our great minds again."

"I think I'll take a quick shower first," I told him as I wrapped a towel around my body, "ALONE this time," I said, pointedly.

"You're no fun," He pouted, grinning.

"That's not what you were saying a little bit ago," I laughingly reminded him, although neither of us needed reminding.

We had just finished our showers and got to the kitchen to start dinner when we heard Kat's happy voice from the yard at the edge of the patio.

Chapter 15

Summer Of Fun

Em '76

Ren, Ray, Chris and I spent as much time together as we possibly could. They even arranged it so Ren and I could work at the same jobs they did. Ren and I worked at jobs that summer we *never* would have imagined ourselves doing. Up to then we had done the 'normal' teenage girl jobs; baby-sitting, light housekeeping, yard mowing and a few other odd jobs. Nothing we had ever done up to that point could have prepared us for the work we did that summer.

That summer found us helping till and plant fields, hauling hay, working at the Bailey sawmill and catching chickens to be sold to large manufacturers then cleaning out some of the chicken houses to prepare them for the next batch of chicks that were to be delivered.

Tilling and planting wasn't too hard with the four of us doing it together. Tilling consisted of two of us driving the tractors while the other two made sure the tractors were working properly; for the planting, two of us would drive the large trucks while the other two made sure the seed was spreading properly. The hardest part of that job for me was the sun. I burned something awful at first.

Hauling hay was a much more physically demanding job for Ren and I, Chris and Ray had been doing it for years so they were used to the physical demands it made on the body but Ren and I thought it was going to kill us! It gave us sore muscles in places we hadn't even known we had muscles! It didn't matter which job you had, whether you were the one following behind the trailer picking up the bales to hand to the person on the trailer, or the one on the trailer being handed the bales to stack neatly on the trailer; both were equally physically demanding tasks. Even driving the trucks that hauled the trailers was hard because the trucks didn't have power steering, and the strain put on the trucks by hauling the heavy trailers made them even harder to steer, two other guys had been hired to drive the trucks. My skin was sore to the touch for *weeks* from the sunburns I got since hauling hay also kept us out in the sun. After a few weeks I finally quit burning and that summer I got the best tan of my life.

The work at the sawmill was hot, hard work but at least it kept us out of the sun most of the time. Usually, we fed wood into the saws, stacked and banded loads to be shipped and helped keep the machinery oiled and running; occasionally though, we would help deliver the stacked, banded wood to local lumber yards and construction sites. At noon, Grandma Bailey would ring the old dinner bell that was hanging just outside the back door of the house and we would all head to the house for a huge meal, then back to the mill as soon as we finished eating.

All of these jobs were dirty, but none of them even came *close* to comparing with the dirty, disgusting job of catching chickens. The first time

Ren and I went with the guys to a large chicken house to catch chickens we had no idea what to expect, or what we were getting into. After that night, we weren't sure we *ever* wanted to do it again. We got dirtier than we'd ever even *wanted* to be, and the *smell*, God the *smell*; it was the worst odor anyone could imagine and then some. To catch the chickens we had to wait until nighttime when they were asleep; then large trucks loaded with crates were backed up to the doors and a black light was turned on in the houses so the chickens wouldn't wake up but the workers could see what they were doing. We would go in, reach under them, grab their legs and carry them upside down to the waiting trucks where we held them up at arms length for the people on the trucks to take and put in the crates. *That's* when the person on the ground got *really messy*, because it scared the shit out of those chickens to feel themselves being shoved up into the air like that. Sometimes, Mom wouldn't even let us in the house until we had hosed ourselves off in the backyard with the water hose. Ren and I decided that even if it *was* the most disgusting job we could ever imagine ourselves doing, at least the pay was pretty good and it meant we could be with Chris and Ray; so we were at least *dirty*, *smelly*, *well-paid*, **happy** people.

Ray's dad owned a large chicken farm so sometimes, after we'd sent the chickens to market we would clean out his houses for the next batch of chicks. The first time we did it he was so happy with our work he teased the guys, saying he wished they would have met us sooner, because he had never seen the houses so clean. We all laughed as the three of them joked back and forth.

When we weren't working, we would either go riding around exploring the countryside or swimming. We usually went swimming in one of two places; either at what had once been an old rock quarry, or the old mill stream.

The water in the quarry was cold and nobody knew exactly how deep it was. There was a spillway at one end that dropped for what seemed like forever before the water from it hit the man made pond below.

The old mill stream was called that because it still had an old paddle mill sitting beside it, with a working paddle wheel. When we were at the stream, it was easy to imagine we had gone back in time at least a hundred years. The water in the stream was spring fed so it was clear, cold and pure. About a hundred yards downstream from the mill was a waterfall. It wasn't a real big waterfall but it was fun to stand under it and feel the water cascading down on you over the falls. Someone had tied a rope to a huge tree beside the stream to be used for swinging out over the water and dropping into it. I never again felt so free as when I was flying through the air waiting to hit the clear, cold water of the stream.

Ren and I didn't spend much time at home that summer, usually if we *were* near the house it was because we were at the pond with Chris and Ray. When we did spend time at the house we would all do things together as a family, Chris and Ray included. Sometimes Mom would pack food and we'd all go to the south side of the pond to picnic, or we'd go places Dad had been as a child growing up in the state or someplace he had heard about at work. A couple of times we went exploring the caves on the East side of the pond, at least until a gigantic snake had paid us a visit in one of them.

Dad had always told us if we ever saw a snake that we were *not* to get excited and start yelling, we should remain calm, and if possible, get as far away from the snake as we could before we made a sound; so when a big snake climbed up on the rock that Karli was sitting on in the cave we were in, she didn't yell, in fact she was so calm that none of us believed her, "Daddy, there's a snake here."   Since she was so calm about it and she didn't to be moving to get away from a snake, none of us paid any attention to her, "Daddy, there's a BIG snake, right beside me." she said again. The third time she said it, Dad looked over at her and saw that there really was a *huge* snake, sitting right beside her on the rock. He ***FREAKED***!!! He yelled, grabbed Karli by the arm and yanked her off the rock, then began blowing the snake to pieces with the gun he had brought along for protection against snakes. Dad was a great shot and never missed what he aimed at, so he killed the snake, but the noise the blast from the gun made inside the small cave was tremendous, almost deafening. He began telling Karli she had done the right thing, and by her not yelling it had probably saved her from getting bitten by the snake, he conveniently left out his own reaction when he had seen the snake beside her. We almost split our sides laughing when Karli said, "But Daddy, I thought you said *nobody* was supposed to make a lot of noise if they saw a snake. You just made a ***lot of noise*** Daddy."

One night I was so sick Ren and I decided we needed to stay home, instead of going out with Chris and Ray. Ren and I spent a lot of time that summer in the camper, (at least when we were home, which wasn't very often;) acting like we were living on our own instead of with our parents. That night we were in the camper and Ren was doing everything she could to make me feel better, or at least doing everything she could to make me laugh. We had a record player in the camper that grandma had gotten me for my twelfth birthday and a record that was called 'The Popcorn Song'; it was a forty five but Ren decided it would sound funnier at seventy eight, so she turned it on at seventy eight RPM's and began making funny faces and moving in time with the music. She was moving so fast, I think she was starting to get dizzy; it was hilarious, but the funniest part was when Chris and Ray came up to the camper window and saw her acting silly and moving fast like that. I thought she was going to just die from the embarrassment.

"How would you all like to go to a Hootenanny on July third, fourth and fifth?" Dad asked us all one evening when he came home from work.

"We might, *if* we knew what the heck it was Dad, it sounds like an owl convention," I didn't care much for owls since I'd had one fly straight at my face the year before when we'd been out hunting one evening. The closer it came, the bigger it's claws seemed to get, finally they each looked a foot long; I heard a gunshot and saw the owl drop at my feet, I stood there shaking, not because Dad had shot the owl so close to my face, I trusted him; but simply because it had *been* so close to my face.

Dad must have known I was thinking about that time, because he reassured me that it was *not* a convention of owls, "It's a three day combination picnic/carnival/fireworks event. I've been to one, but it was a long time ago, my mom and dad took my brothers and sister and I to one in Mountain Home. It was a lot of fun then and since things don't seem to change much around here, I'm sure it will be just as much fun now as it was back in 'the good old days'," we laughed at his joke, especially Karli, because she thought anybody over thirty was ancient. "we'll be staying all three days so we'll be taking the camper and some sleeping bags."

"At least it will only be three days this time, not three months," Mom cut in. We all laughingly agreed with her.

"Oh, Em and Ren, if it's alright with their parents and they can get the time off work, Chris and Ray can go with us too."

"Thanks, Dad, we'll ask them and we'll get the time off work too. It sounds like it's going to be a lot of fun." Chris and Ray were already on their way over, so we would tell them when they got here.

Chris and Ray were as excited about the news as we were and both of them called their parents from our house. Chris' mom said it was fine with her and Ray's parents said that as long as our parents were going to be there, it would be okay if he went too.

"Good, it's all settled then, we'll leave the afternoon of the second so we'll be sure to get a good campsite. Somewhere we don't have to walk a mile or more to get to the festivities."

For something that had such a strange name, the hootenanny turned out to be a lot of fun. It was at a place called Sugar Loaf Mountain beside a lake and it didn't take long to get there, even hauling the camper. Chris and Ray's parents all said it was fine with them if they went since our parents would be there, so Ren and I rode down with them in Ray's car. Dad parked the truck with the camper on it in a campground next to the lake. It was beautiful there, there was an island in the middle of the lake with a ferry that went back and forth four times an hour.

The Hootenanny turned out to be like a huge carnival; complete with rides, cotton candy and hot dog stands everywhere, clowns and tightrope walkers, elephants and tigers; everything you would expect to see at a huge carnival, my personal favorite though was a giant carousel in the middle of it all. I had loved calliope music since I'd first heard it when I was about three years old. Ren and I didn't see much of our family the first day, we spent it with Chris and Ray; exploring, riding all the rides, playing the games in the booths, riding the ferry to the mountain in the middle of the lake, eating everything in sight and enjoying the scenery.

That night was when the real fun began. A stage had been set up by the shores of the lake and a well known country band took the stage and invited anyone who wanted to sing to come on up. Mom loved to sing so she decided to go up on the stage with them. At first she was nervous but soon she had everyone stomping their feet and clapping their hands; keeping time with the music and singing along. Ren and I finally joined her onstage and we all sang some old Loretta Lynn and Patsy Cline songs. They were Mom's favorite singers so we had grown up with their music, as well as those of other country artists. I had never seen my mom enjoy herself as much as she did that night.

The next two days flew by in a jumble of fun; fireworks, picnics, singing every night, riding the rides and just all around having the time of our lives. All too soon it was over and time to go home. Mom never stopped talking about it after that and Dad said that while he had known she could sing, he didn't know she could sing as good as she had with the bands in those three nights. We all laughed when he told Ren and I that we must have gotten our singing abilities from our mother, because he sure couldn't sing.

That summer may have been the hardest I ever worked, but it was also turning out to be the *best* summer of my life.

Chapter 16

Recruiting

Chris '96

"You were right about them having no will of their own and no sense of humor, they acted kind of like the zombies in the old movies." I thought for a minute, then said excitedly, "do you know what they really remind me of? That movie 'Invasion Of The Body Snatchers'; you know, the one about the pod people taking over human bodies, leaving them with no emotions at all. It starred Donald Sutherland, Leonard Nimoy and Brooke something or other," I couldn't ever remember her name because her acting had never impressed me much.

"Yeah, now that you mention it, that's what they remind me of too. I remember the movie, I watched it because it had Leonard Nimoy in it, you know how I am when it comes to anything that has anyone from Star Trek in it, especially Leonard Nimoy, he's always been one of my favorite actors."

"Do I remember? How could I forget Chris??" Smiling, "I think we watched every episode together at least fifty times the summer I moved here," we laughed at the memory. Sci-fi and horror were one of the many things we'd always had in common. "Speaking of Star Trek, I can't believe you've still got every one of those autographed pictures we got that summer." We had started a local Star Trek fan club that summer and had gotten autographed pictures of all the major stars and most of the minor ones. Chris had framed each one of them and they were now hanging on the walls of his study at home.

"What can I say, I'm a die hard Trekkie," he laughed.

"So am I, thanks to you," I smiled at him, "but enough about the good old days, what's the game plan for this evening's visits? Who are the people we'll be trying to convince? How many are there and how much luck do you think we'll have with them?"

"There are five new families, including the Abbott's, each with a varying number of family members. All the committee members were told the names of all the new people. That way we could all check each of them out, get their reasons for not going to the council meetings, compare notes to see if we all got the same stories from them, then give our report at the next council meeting."

"When is the next town council meeting?"

"In a week, which gives us a little time but I want to be the first to approach as many of them as we can to determine if they're infected or not. If they are, we'll simply make our excuses and move on to the next family."

"It makes me feel so helpless, knowing we can't help them all."

"I know the feeling, believe me, I've been dealing with it for years."

"I don't know how you've dealt with it all these years alone. I don't know if I could have done it alone. I would have been scared to death."

"I was scared most of the time, so I dealt with it the only way I could, by telling myself I was quite possibly the only hope any of those people not infected had of getting free of the evil before it took them over completely, or got them killed. It hasn't been easy, believe me. I've only been able to save a few. You have no idea how difficult it is telling someone who doesn't know you from Adam that there is some kind of evil force controlling the area. I've gotten some strange looks, let me tell you."

"I can imagine. How in the world do you bring the subject up, without sounding like an escapee from a lunatic asylum?"

"It varies from family to family. At least now that we know about the anemia and infected beef we have a better starting point than I've had in the past."

"I guess I'm about to find out what it's like to be looked at like I'm an escaped lunatic," I said as we pulled into the driveway of the first family on the list. He smiled, grimly. I could tell these visits were not his idea of a good time. I dreaded going to the door, anticipating the reception we would get.

"That wasn't *quite* as bad as I thought it would be," I grimaced as we had the door shut firmly behind us by an emotionless man named John Brady and his wife Ellen. He had told us his truck was broken down and they hadn't been able to get to town for the meeting, but he had made arrangements to get a ride to town for the meetings from now on if they had any more problems with his truck. "We can scratch one family from our list of those we can still help, huh," as we got back in the truck.

"Yeah, they're beyond our reach already. The power of the evil is beginning to infect people faster than it has in the past. He said they have only been here for a little over a month. It used to take at least six months for them to get as far gone as those two are," he put his head in his hands, "God, sometimes it seems so useless!" He looked suddenly tired and the fine lines beside his mouth deepened as his lips compressed into a hard, straight line.

"Maybe the next house won't be as bad," I comforted him, "at least we can hope that's the case." Silently, I doubted the truth of my words.

"Ever the optimist, huh Em. That's one of the things I've always loved about you. We better get going, it really is starting to get late now, but if we hurry we can get to two more of the names on the list before we head home."

"Where's the nearest one?"

"About two miles down this road, then left another quarter of a mile."

"So, what are we waiting for? Let's get going."

Laughing at my enthusiasm, he started the truck, "Okey-Dokey partner."

"Okey-Dokey?" I grinned.

"Kat's not the only one who watches too much television sometimes," he informed me.

The couple in the second house turned out to be quite a bit more infected than the first, and were way too far gone for us to do them any good. We left with their assurances that they would definitely be at the next town council meeting, they would have attended this evening's meeting but their only daughter had gotten married today in Little Rock and they hadn't been able to make it back from the wedding in time. They showed us part of a video of what seemed to be a very nice wedding, though they, as the parents of the bride, seemed to stay strangely emotionless throughout the entire thing. We thanked them for their time then headed back out to the truck.

"What did you think?"

"Not a chance. Any mother who can sit through her only daughter saying 'I DO' without showing any emotion at all is WAY beyond help," I shook my head in disbelief, "Thank God for anemia, and thank my mother for not wanting us to eat beef the whole time I was growing up, I don't ever want to be that emotionally …. dead! The people we've seen so far this evening are like emotional wastelands!!"

"I agree, totally! Last one on the list for this evening is," he glanced at the list in his hands, "the Abbott's, who happen to be my neighbors. My closest neighbors anyway, their house is about two and a half miles North of mine."

"Abbott? I heard that name mentioned earlier this evening too. I thought maybe I remembered the name from school. Weren't there some twins named Abbott in our class? Jared and … damn, what's her name?"

"Janel. Yeah that's them. Janel went to California to be an actress; Jared married Carrie Eaton, they both became architects and moved to New York. They worked in some hotshot architectural firm there for a while before starting their own practice. His parents passed away a few years ago and he asked me to keep an eye on the homeplace for them until they could sell it. I thought they priced it way too high for this area though and so far it hasn't sold. He told me when they moved to New York that they didn't ever want to come back because most of the people around here were just too damn weird for them. Then about six weeks ago, I got a call from Carrie, telling me Jared had suffered from some kind of attack of severe stress. She told me the doctors said he would be fine but that he needed to slow down before he had another attack, or worse yet, a heart attack. She seemed to be really worried about him and they discussed their options and finally decided that even though they didn't really want to, they didn't have a lot of options and they would move back into the old family home down here, where life was more laid back. They just started moving back in about four days ago." He cleared his throat, "God Em, how are we going to tell them they would have been better off staying in New York?" He signaled for the turn that would take us to the Abbott's home.

"I don't know Chris, but we've got to warn them about what's been going on around here and if they aren't infected yet, see if they may be able to help us in some way," I said as we pulled to a stop in front of the farmhouse, "You know, it will be nice to see them again. Carrie was my best friend in school here," I reached out to touch his arm, "besides you that is. She was always nuts, hyper as hell, never able to sit still for very long, always moving around from one thing to another. She used to make me tired just watching her." We laughed as we remembered how Carrie had been in school. She had been like a whirlwind in those days. "I just wish our reunion were under better circumstances."

"I know what you mean. She always made me tired just watching her too. She was a nut, wasn't she? It's been a while since I've seen them too. The last time was three years ago when I took a trip to New York for a seminar on horses. She was still her old nutty self when I was in New York, let's hope she still is." He knocked on the door of Jared and Carrie's home. I reached out for his hand just before the door opened.

Chapter 17

Evil Comes To Call

Both - '96

"That was fun! When can we go again? I can't wait to tell Mommy about that **GIANT** bullfrog we saw!!" She chattered, as they stopped halfway across the patio, "And Daddy too." Her voice lowered a little as she said the last part, as if she still found it hard to believe she had finally found him. "And did you see all those snakes?! YUCK, I hate snakes!! They're creepy!!"

Chris' head snapped around at the mention of snakes, "It's starting to escalate already. I didn't think it would happen so fast. God, I'm not ready for it to be going this fast yet."

"I need to mention the snakes to Dad, I've never seen so many of them in one place before, but he has," Kim said, more to herself than anyone else; then "by the way, talking about giant bullfrogs, have you guys ever had frogs legs before?" She asked my kids.

"Uh-huh, once. I watched Mommy cook them too. They tried to jump out of the pan," Kat told her.

"It was cool!!" Joe put in, "The way they jumped around in the skillet like that."

"It was gross!!" Kat turned to whisper to Kim, (the way most five year olds do, *loudly*) "I don't think they were dead all the way when Mommy put 'em in the pan Kim." I smiled at the memory of how upset she had been with me for cooking what she thought were live frogs. I tried to tell her they were dead, they had to be because they weren't hooked to the frogs anymore, but she had never really believed it. She reminded me so much of Karli when she did things like that.

Kim took Kat's hand and bent down, "No hon, they *were* dead all the way; it's just that if the tendons aren't cut right the legs seem to jump around in the pan. I thought the same thing the first time I saw them cooked when the tendons weren't cut right, but they *really were dead.* They weren't hooked to the frogs any more so they had to be dead, right? A frog leg can't live without the rest of the frog."

"OK," she said, (in a voice that suggested she thought Kim was *probably* right, which meant I must have been too when I'd told her they were dead,) "Then I guess maybe I should apologize to Mommy for not believing her when she told me they *were* dead, huh."

"Chris, what were you whispering about?" He didn't seem to hear me, "Chris? Chris!!" I shook his shoulder, which, after a few moments seemed to break the trance he appeared to be in, causing him to look at me, "WHAT were you whispering about Chris?"

"The snakes Em, the SNAKES!! You heard what they just said about the number of snakes down at the lake. It's escalating faster than I thought it would. Remember what I told you about the snakes and spiders?" Just then the door opened, "We'll continue this conversation later," he said quickly, just as Kat came rushing in.

"Mommy, you should have seen the bullfrog we saw. It was bigger than a kitty!!" She said, exaggerating, as she sometimes tended to do, especially when she was overly excited about something. She saw the look of amused disbelief on my face, "OK, maybe not *bigger* than a kitty, but it was sure close! It was the biggest one in the world! I just know it was!!!"

"It sure must have been a big one to get you so excited, munchkin," Chris said as he picked her up and swung her up onto his shoulders. I smiled as I heard him use the pet name I had for her. She squealed with joy.

"Oh it *WAS*!!!" she said happily, "Daddy." The last word was said quietly and proudly.

"OK, midget," I told her as I finished setting the table, "Enough about frogs and kitties for now, have your dad take you to wash up for dinner." She smiled when I called Chris her dad.

"Ok, Mommy. Giddy-up, Daddy!" She laughed as he whinnied then galloped out of the kitchen.

"I haven't seen Dad this happy since before Mom died," Kim said as she helped me put the food on the table, before she went to wash up for dinner.

Chloe got the salad out of the refrigerator, setting it on the counter, "I don't think I've *ever* seen Kat this happy!" She smiled as she turned to go get cleaned up for dinner.

After dinner, Chris gave the kids some money so they could go to see a movie in Batesville. After promising to watch Kat closely, they all climbed into Kim's car and headed for Batesville. When they'd gone, I made us each a glass of iced tea and we went out to sit on the covered glider on the patio.

"Now we can finish our earlier conversation." I said as I turned to face Chris, waiting for the explanation of why he had seemed to go into a trance earlier.

"Well, you heard what Kat and Kim said about snakes right? A *LOT* of snakes! That's how it was the last time, twenty-five years ago. Snakes multiplying at a rate ten times faster than normal, they were everywhere Em, everywhere."

"Yes, I heard them mention it and I remember you telling me the other day about the spiders and snakes from twenty-five years ago. Do you really think it's gotten to that point so soon?"

"Yes, I do. I think whenever there's a big event concerning the 'master' the snakes begin multiplying faster and the spiders get bigger and there are more of them. Twenty-five years ago when the 'master' was put in to Bailey's Pond to incubate it happened; and now that it's getting ready to hatch, or whatever the hell it's called, it's happening again. It seems that things concerning it/him, whatever it is, happen in twenty-five year cycles. Now, if we can just figure out how to stop it from growing."

"My God, Chris, if that's the case something should happen again in twenty-five years!"

"*Something* probably will, unless we can stop it now. I don't know if that will do any good though, because we don't even know what all was put in that pond. Damn!! What the hell do we do next?!?!"

"Maybe we should check the local papers to see if there have been an unusually large number of snakebite cases lately, as well as a large number of unexplained deaths."

"What would I do without you to keep me sane, woman?" He said as he rose to go in to the living room to get the day's paper that no-one as yet had bothered to read. He stopped just before entering the house and turned to look at me, "I know exactly what I'd do. I'd go out of my freaking mind!" He continued on in to the house, returning a few moments later scanning through the days paper and carrying the ones from the past week. "You were right Em," he said as he sat down, "There were five people admitted to the hospital for snakebite, and that's just in today's paper. Three have died so far and the doctors say the standard antivenin used for cases like these isn't working on the remaining patients; they don't believe the other two will make it either. The reporter says there have been more instances of snakebite in the area in the last week, twenty five so far, than there have been in almost thirty years. It says here that the last time there were this many cases of snakebite in such a short period of time, in which the antivenin was *also ineffective*, with *all* the victims dying, was in 1971." He looked over at me, "Which was the year that man showed up at the town meeting."

Just then we heard the doorbell, Chris and I both went to answer it. When Chris opened the door we saw Mr. Graves standing there.

"I don't mean to intrude," he said to Chris, "but I have someone here who would like to speak to you and Em," as he moved aside, another man stepped into the doorway. It was the same man Chris had described to me from the town meeting twenty-five years earlier! The man with **BLACK EYES**!!!!

Chapter 18

Academic Life

Em '76

The weeks following the hootenanny were filled with a lot of work as well as fun. Harvest was in full swing so we were kept pretty busy in the fields but we still made time to have fun. Chris and Ray showed us how to gig frogs, where a long pole with a little pitchfork looking thing on the end is used to spear frogs. Around there it was called 'friggin', a combination of the two words 'frog giggin'. It was messy, but kind of fun. Where we'd come from, friggin' meant something completely different, so the first time we came home and told Mom we'd been out friggin', she started sputtering, we quickly explained to her what it was, before she could start yelling for Dad. Mom cooked the frogs we caught and even though we didn't think we would, we liked the taste. Once, when some of them weren't cut right, they started jumping around in the pan. Karli accused us of cooking live frogs and wouldn't eat them for a long time after that.

Before we knew it, August was halfway over and school would be starting in a few weeks. Mom took Jace and Karli to Mountain Home, Calico Rock and Batesville to shop for school supplies and new clothes. Ren and I used some of the money we had earned over the summer, (which turned out to be quite a lot of money) to buy our own stuff and Chris and Ray took us shopping.

Chris and Ray took Ren and I to enroll. Chris and I would be sophomores so we got to take most of our classes together, except for P.E., auto shop and home-economics, those classes still had boys and girls separated, at least in the smaller Arkansas towns. They were required course so we had to take them, but we let the teachers know we didn't like it that they still thought boys and girls needed to be separated for those classes. I started a petition that said the only places boys and girls should be separated was in the locker rooms and restrooms; because it wasn't likely that the boys wouldn't need to know how to cook and sew, or that the girls wouldn't need to know the basics of car repair. Every student in the high school, junior high and the upper grades of the elementary signed it, as well as most of the teachers and parents. It went to the school board and passed, mainly because the board meeting was filled with students, teachers and parents who supported the petition. Of course I wasn't very popular with those still opposed to it, the few who didn't want things to change. I had always been one to stand up for what I believed in however, even if it meant I was labeled an opinionated, outspoken troublemaker. While I may have *been* all those things, I tended to get things done. I didn't give up on things I believed strongly about, no matter how much trouble I got into.

While the petition *DID* pass the board, it was decided that it wouldn't be put into effect until the following school year so it would cause the least amount of upheaval as possible. I was happy with that, knowing things *would* be changing, for the better.

The rest of my classes I spent with Chris in them. I was really good at English, History, Geography and Spelling while he was good at Math and Science courses. We helped each other and did well in all our classes. The lowest grade I got that year was a B, (except for biology) which was in math because I still had a hard time comprehending algebra. I was happy with that grade though because up until that year the highest grade I'd gotten in math was a C-. My parents were thrilled.

Ren and Ray, both seniors, both had only one required course left to take, Government; the rest were electives, so all of their classes were together. Jace was in the eighth grade now and was just happy she was that much closer to high school, which meant she was that much closer to being a senior, so she was that much closer to getting out of school. Totally unlike Jace, Karli was thrilled to be able to go to school. She got up every morning excited and happy, (which made Jace sick) hurrying to get dressed and ready for school so she could learn more. She reminded me a lot of myself, both of us excited to learn new things. I believed that knowledge was power and a person should never stop learning or stop being willing to learn. Karli, as young as she was, understood and agreed with that.

Ren and I, though neither one tall, were both fast, so we joined the girls basketball team that year. We were never great, but we had fun playing. I had more fun that school year than I ever had in school before.

Biology was the class I liked the least because we had to dissect animals. Even though they were dead I didn't like the idea of cutting them up *or* the smell of formaldehyde. The teacher, Mr. Graves, couldn't understand how anyone could *not* like it, but he was a jerk (and I suspected privately, a sadist, since he seemed to get a kick out of seeing students get sick when they had to cut open a frog or a piglet.) One day he told the class he was working with the University of Arkansas to arrange a special treat for us, he said he was pretty sure he would be able to get some human fetuses for us to dissect. I'd never liked the man but when he said that I decided I'd had enough!! I stood up and said that I, as a female who would one day probably be giving *birth* to human fetuses did *not* want to see one in a jar of formaldehyde, *nor* did I particularly want to see what they looked like on the inside. I told him I *refused* to take part in his class if he was going to try to get us to do something so disgusting!! He could flunk me if he wanted to, but he would **never** get me to do that. I picked up my books and walked out of the room. As I was walking out the door I heard people clapping behind me, I turned and saw all but one of the students standing, applauding me, (the guy still seated was one of those people who will do whatever they're told to keep out of trouble, no matter what it was). The students who were standing all picked up their books and followed me.

We went straight to the principals office. I explained what Mr. Graves had said and my response to it. I told the principal that even if I flunked the class, I would **not** do what Mr. Graves had planned for the class. The other students told him they felt the same way. Mr. Graves showed up after we'd explained how we felt to Mr. Mobley. He told Mr. Mobley that he would not put up with his class striking and walking out on him like we had done. Mr. Mobley told him he was more inclined to agree with the students, He told Mr. Graves that this was NOT medical school, it was high school and that he didn't think we could, or for that matter, even *should*, be made to dissect a human fetus. He also said he that even if we *could* be made to do it, he would side with us against it because we felt so strongly about it. Graves was mad as hell about Mr. Mobley's decision but knew he didn't have any choice in the matter. He said okay, that was fine, we *wouldn't* be dissecting a human fetus but he was going to keep a close eye on everyone who had walked out of his class that day, *especially me.* I didn't care if he kept an eye on me or not, as long as our class wasn't going to have to dissect a human fetus. I returned to class, with the rest of the students following me. I spent the rest of that school year with Graves *severely* disliking me and doing all he could to get me in trouble with Mr. Mobley, as well as in trouble with the rest of the teachers. Needless to say, my grade in the class never got above a C. I didn't care about my grade however because while I may not have won the war, I had at least won that battle.

Mt. Pleasant was a small school with the largest class that year being the senior class. Usually only the junior class got to decorate for the prom but due to the *large* number of seniors compared to the *small* number of juniors that year, the faculty decided to allow the sophomores help the juniors decorate. Which meant the sophomores could also *go* to the prom. The whole sophomore class was excited by the news *and* thankful for the large number of students in the senior class.

Chapter 19

Balance

Chris '96

"Chris, this is quite a surprise." Carrie stood framed in the light of the doorway, "Jared and I were just talking about you." She still hadn't noticed me, standing to the side, in the dark beside him.

"None of it good, I suppose." He joked.

"Oh, you!" She laughed as she moved aside for him to come in. We were still holding hands so as he moved to go in the house, it pulled me into the light from the doorway. "Em!!" She squealed, grabbing me to hug me, "My God, is it really you? We haven't seen each other for ages, let me look at you!!" she held me away from her so she could get a better look at me, "Woman do you *ever* age? You look just like you did on your first book cover, four… no, it was five, years ago."

I laughed at her enthusiastic welcome, "That's when the book came out but the picture was actually a few years old at the time."

""Don't *even* tell me that, because it means you look even better than I thought," she laughed as she pulled us both inside, "Jared will be so happy to see you both. Excuse the mess but as I'm sure Chris has told you, we're just now moving in. Jared's in the study, so if you two can still find your way to the deck, I'll go get him and bring him out. It is SO good to see you again Em." She went to get Jared as Chris and I made our way out to the deck.

"She hasn't changed a bit," I said as we sat in the deck chairs. "Still just as nutty as ever."

"Yes, thank God. That means she's not infected either."

"I know, I'm so glad."

"It really *is* you," we stood as we heard the deep voice from the doorway, "when Carrie told me Chris had brought you over, my mind jumped back in time twenty years. You two seemed to be joined at the hip back then," seeing we were holding hands, he laughed, "Some things never change, huh." He's reached us by that time, "Come here, you," he grabbed me and hugged me as Carrie had done at the front door. "It's really good to see you again Em. You have been busy, haven't you? We read your first book when it came out five years ago and we've read every one since. I bet your agent's happy, what with at least one book a year and sometimes as many as three."

"You've read *all* my books?" I could hardly believe it.

"Oh yes, you're quite a good writer. Carrie's favorites are the ones in the series about the nun who's an amateur sleuth. I prefer the sci-fi myself but I enjoy the nun series too."

"I'm stunned!" I sat down, heavily.

"You shouldn't be, you really are a good writer. Besides, in school you *were* the one voted to have the best imagination."

Carrie laughed, "*And* voted the most opinionated and outspoken. Do you guys remember the time she got all but one of the students to get up and walk out of Graves' biology class because he said we might be dissecting a human fetus that year?" She laughed, "Boy was he ever pissed about it, I don't think he ever did get over that one. He was such a jerk!"

"He still is," I told her.

"You've seen him?"

"Oh yeah, just a little while ago Carrie, at the town meeting."

"That's sort of why we're here," Chris put in, "We need to talk to you guys about something that's been going on around here. Something that's hard to believe. I've been living with it for years and sometimes I still have a hard time believing it."

"Does it have anything to do with Bailey's Pond?"

Chris looked quickly at Jared, "You know about it?"

"We don't know *exactly* what's going on, but we knew enough to scare us off a long time ago. Remember, I told you before we left that most of the people around here were just too weird for us? That was part of it, but the main reason was the evil spreading throughout the area. I never said anything to anyone because I was afraid people would think I was crazy, or worse yet, that someone would tell the man with the black eyes about me. If you'll remember Chris I was at that town meeting twenty five years ago too. I'm glad I can finally talk about it; to someone other than Carrie that is."

"I thought I was the only one who knew and wasn't infected by it and here you've suspected something was happening all along," Chris sighed with relief, then a puzzled expression crossed his face, "But, if you know about it, then you must realize what's been going on around here lately and yet you still came back. WHY?"

"To kick it's ass!!" We all laughed at the force Jared put into his words, "When we heard about the snake population increasing so rapidly, we suspected something was going to happen. The news made me think of that town meeting and about that man with the black eyes, which brought back everything he told the people at that council meeting about the plague of spiders and snakes that had brought him to the meeting in the first place. We didn't think you were infected, but we couldn't be sure; when you came to visit us in New York, you seemed fine Chris, but we thought it might be because you were so far away from the evil. So, when Carrie called to tell you we were coming back, we made up the stress attack thing. Sorry we had to lie to you, but we had to be completely sure. The only way we could do that was to see you here, in the middle of it all. You know how it is."

"Do I ever!! I understand why you couldn't tell me the truth, no problem there, don't give it a second thought. I would have done the same thing if I had been in your shoes," Chris assured them both, "Do you eat meat?" He asked them.

The question surprised them because it seemed to come out of thin air. Carrie answered for both of them, "Some pork, lamb and seafood, but not beef. Why?"

"I didn't think so," he said, more to himself than the rest of us; to them, "We eat pork, lamb and seafood too, but not beef." Then another question seeming to come from nowhere, "So, are either of you anemic?"

"Yes, we both are. Jared more than me, but not too much more. Why? What are you getting at Chris?"

"Our aversion to eating beef and the anemia seem to be our reasons for being immune. Our blood isn't rich enough to satisfy the evils' hunger, so it leaves us alone."

"That's what protects us from it? I always wondered why some people didn't seem to be as infected as others were."

I happened to notice the clock on the wall, "Chris, I hate to break up the party, but it's almost nine thirty. Kat will want to hear a story before she goes to sleep and the rest of the kids are probably wondering where we are."

"Kat? Your daughter Em?" Carrie asked as we all walked toward the front door.

"Actually Carrie, she's *our* daughter," Chris told her. A look of confusion came over her face.

"How old is she?"

"Five. It's a long story Carrie."

"Why don't you guys come over for dinner tomorrow and we'll tell you all about it," I offered, then looked over at Chris, "Would you look at me? Here I am inviting people over to your house without even bothering to ask you. Aren't I just the pushy one?"

He laughed, "I don't mind. If you hadn't asked them over I would have." He reached for my hand again, "Would eleven be alright with you guys?" He asked them.

"Sure, and I want the *whole story* Em." Carrie said, smiling, hugging us both just before we went outside.

"You'll get it Carrie. I promise we'll tell you the entire story."

As we started for home Chris said "You know, it's strange knowing I *wasn't* the only one who knew about everything that has been going on all this time. With their help, *maybe* the balance will shift a little in our favor. At least I hope so."

"So do I Chris, so do I."

Chapter 20

At Risk

Both '96

I couldn't believe the man was actually *here*, standing in the doorway looking at us, with black eyes. I felt Chris reach out to take my hand. Chris had been right when he had told me the man's eyes were in some strange way, hypnotic. I fought hard to keep the shock and fear I was feeling from showing in my face, as well as to keep myself from staring at the mans eyes. As I looked over at Chris I knew he was trying to do the same thing. I could tell by the tight, trembling grip he had on my hand. His face however, betrayed none of what I knew he had to be feeling. I could only hope I was even half as successful at concealing my shock and fear at seeing the man here as he was.

"Chris, Em, I'd like to introduce Mr. Jeffers," I heard Mr. Graves tell us.

"Please, call me Will," Jeffers said, putting out his gloved hand for us to shake, ('Gloves? In this heat?' I felt myself wondering) "It's Willard actually but I've never cared much for the name, I prefer Will," by the way he said it I could tell he was a man who was used to getting what he wanted, as Chris forced himself to shake the offered hand. As Chris still had my right hand gripped tightly in his left, I was spared having to touch Jeffers, at least for the moment.

"As I said, Mr. Jeffers would like to speak with both of you," Graves repeated, "It's a matter of the utmost importance, I can assure you. May we come in?"

"Of course, I'm sorry, do come in," Chris and I stepped aside to allow the two men to come in, "We were out back on the patio, would you like to join us out there?"

"Certainly," Jeffers said, "lead the way."

"It's this way," Chris said as we walked toward the sliding doors that led to the patio.

I finally found my voice after they'd seated themselves at the patio table near the glider, "Would you like something to drink? We were having iced tea." My voice only trembled slightly. 'Not *too* bad' I thought to myself, 'considering I feel as if I'm about to pass out'. Aloud, I said, "It wouldn't be any trouble getting two more glasses for you, if you'd like some."

"As long as you feel it won't be any bother, that would be nice. This heat *is* something, isn't it?" Jeffers glanced at me, then looked off toward the lake.

Chris still had a firm grip on my hand, "I'll help you Em." As we made our way to the kitchen for their tea, his grip loosened slightly; I pulled my hand from his, my fingers tingling as feeling began returning to them.

"I wonder what he wants with us?" I murmured as I rubbed my hand, which was red from being gripped so tightly.

Chris noticed me rubbing my hand and saw how red it was, he reached out for it, "Hon, I'm sorry, did I hurt you? I didn't mean to, it was just such a shock seeing him at the door like that. He's never been to my house before."

He took my hand in both of his and rubbed it until all the feeling returned and the redness was gone.

"No, it's fine. I was shocked too. I'll be fine, at least my hand will." I hugged him, got the glasses from the cabinet then went to get the ice from the freezer while he got the tea from the refrigerator. "Besides, I think I was squeezing your hand just as tight as you were squeezing mine, although I'm not *quite* as strong as you are." I smiled, letting him know I was teasing. I could see the concern for me still on his face however, so I reassured him "Chris, my hand is fine, really." 'I just wish the same could be said for my mind,' I thought to myself.

"OK, but I'm still sorry I squeezed it so hard," he said as he poured the tea into the tall glasses I'd put ice in. He put the pitcher back in the refrigerator as I picked up the glasses to take outside. Just before we headed back out, he leaned over to quickly kiss me, "Together, we can handle this," he said just before opening the door to the patio.

"I know Chris. Together, we can handle anything." We stepped out onto the patio, "Here you go," I said as I handed the two men their tea.

"Thank you," as they each took their glasses.

Chris and I got our tea from beside the glider and joined them at the table, "Now, what was it you wanted to discuss, Mr. Jeffers?" Chris looked at Jeffers. I could tell it was hard for him to look at the man with out staring at his black eyes.

"Please, *do* call me Will."

"OK, Will, what was it you wanted to discuss with us?"

"Your daughter, Kat."

I swear my heart stopped beating when he said it. They *knew* Kat was Chris' daughter, as well as mine. I knew now *why* Graves had known about

Chris and I seeing each other again in Vegas in '90, and I knew why I'd wondered at the time if our meeting again after all that time had been coincidence or some greater force at work. It apparently had *not* been coincidence.

Somehow I found my voice and forced myself to ask, "Our *daughter*?" My voice shook slightly. I looked over at Chris, knowing his thoughts were running wild, wondering *why* this man knew about Kat; and *how* he knew, when he himself had just recently found out. I shook my head slightly, as if to say I had no idea how the hell he knew either. Chris must have known that's what I was thinking because he reached out to take my hand again, gently this time.

"What about her?" Chris wanted to know. I wanted to ask the same question, but I didn't trust my voice not to betray my feelings, so I kept silent, for the moment.

"She needs to be prepared."

"Prepared? Prepared for what?"

"Her future, with the 'master'."

"Her future? With the 'master'?" Chris sounded like a parrot, repeating every word Jeffers said.

"Of course, I thought you'd been told," he looked over at Graves with a look on his face that defied description, "you didn't *tell* them?"

"I haven't had the opportunity." I thought I saw a flicker of fear in his eyes as he admitted his failure.

"Exactly *what* are you two talking about?" Chris asked, trying to control the anger I knew he was feeling, on top of a deep fear for Kat's safety.

Jeffers then confirmed one of my worst fears, "Your meeting in '90 was **not** simply mere coincidence. You were chosen, by the 'master'. Chosen, by the way, because of your abilities to avoid his power *to some extent*." Chris and I looked quickly at each other; apparently, while they *did* know we were partially immune, they *didn't* know Chris and I were *TOTALLY IMMUNE* to the evil infecting nearly everyone else in the area. "Abilities you apparently both acquired by your aversion to eating beef and being anemic." I silently thanked my Mom for giving me the aversion to beef he was talking about, then thanked both my parents for giving me the genes that cause anemia.

"Chosen to do *what*?" Chris asked as his grip on my hand slowly began to tighten, I wiggled my fingers and the pressure eased up a little. I couldn't have said a word if I'd had to, I was in shock.

""To breed and produce a mate for the 'master'. He wanted a mate that would not be totally consumed by his power, one who would be immune to the evils visited on the others. You've noticed, I'm sure that your combined families are the only ones, of those who have been here a while, even remotely immune to him in this area. The only ones he's allowed to *survive*, that is. The reason for that was to keep his mate happy. She wouldn't have been very happy if members of her family had suddenly started dying, now would she. I'm told she is a very happy, well adjusted child." Smiling, he paused to take a drink of his tea, then continued, "The time has now come for you, her parents, to know. As well as to show you what you'll need to teach her to prepare her for when the time comes that the 'master' will take her as his mate."

Chris' hand tightened around mine again, but as I was in shock due to Jeffers latest declaration, I felt no pain. I felt nothing; nothing but a huge sense of dread. I could not believe this was happening. 'It *can't* be happening!! Things like this just don't happen in the 90's. The *1690's maybe*, but **NOT** the *1990's*,' I thought to myself, or at least *tried* to think. My fear was quickly making me incapable of *any* rational thought.

"And *who* will teach us to do that?" I heard Chris ask, his voice shaking slightly. He cleared his throat in an attempt to control his anger, then continued, his voice a little more steady, "What will we need to know? What will *she* need to know? *When* will the 'master' take her as his mate?" I could feel the anger he was trying so hard to keep inside threatening to spill out, making it impossible for him to continue and forced myself to ask, my voice quite a few octaves higher than normal, "When will we meet the 'master'?"

"So many questions. The 'master' will be pleased at the interest you've shown," he apparently had mistaken our angry questions for interest, (which was probably better for us, judging by what happened to those considered a threat to the 'master'). "I'm afraid we're out of time right now, but we will be in touch tomorrow and I will try to answer the questions you've asked so far as well as the other questions I'm sure you'll have by then. Thank you for your time, understanding and interest. We'll see ourselves out. Until tomorrow then." He motioned Graves to stand and they made their way to the front door.

After we heard them drive away Chris and I looked at each other and said in unison, "MY GOD, they want Kat!!" Then neither of us said anything for a while, both too shocked by everything Jeffers had told us.

Finally his anger broke free, "Prepare her for a future with the 'master', my ass! Not in this lifetime!! I'll be damned if I'll let them have her! She's ours and there's no way they're getting her! I'll do whatever it takes to keep her from them!! My God, Em, they think we'll just blindly follow their plans to mate her with that damn thing!!! Whatever the hell it is!!"

When I could speak again, "We've got to kill it Chris!! Somehow, we've got to figure out how to kill the 'master'! I will NOT let it have our daughter! No way in hell!!!" I stood, heading for the house and the phone, "I'm calling Jared and Carrie, we're going to need help."

"All the help we can get." Chris jumped from his chair to follow me in to make the call. "I don't believe this is happening!!"

Chapter 21

Prom Night '77

Em '77

Throughout the entire school year the three upper grades did whatever we could think of to raise money for the senior prom. We had bake sales, carnivals and yard sales; held raffles with the winner receiving something or other one of our parents or grandparents had either just wanted to get rid of or had made, like quilts or afghans and things like that; we made items in wood shop and sold them at craft fairs; put on plays and hosted chili suppers.

When the time came to prepare and decorate for the prom, we had earned so much money that we had enough extra to pay for the senior trip and were able to take the sophomore, junior and senior classes as well as their teachers to see two plays at the University in Batesville. We saw wonderful local productions of 'Bus Stop' and 'Dracula'.

Suggestions were made by the senior class to decide what their prom's theme would be, then the suggestions were voted on, with the one getting the most votes winning. The winning theme turned out to be 'Time In A Bottle'.

The decorating committee was let out of school the day before the prom, which was to be held on a Saturday, and spent the entire day decorating the gym for the seniors. Of course the committee used the school colors in the decorating; blue and white streamers were hung from the ceiling, the top half of the walls were strung with small blue and white lights twinkling behind white netting, while the lower half of the wall was covered with a long strip of rolled construction paper on which the seniors had all written their names, as well as their plans for the future. Outside, the walkway leading to the gymnasium was strung with blue and white lights behind white netting also. We had talked Mr. Graves into getting us some dry ice so we could create a smoky, dreamlike setting.

Long tables were set up around the room for the dinner and awards ceremony that was to be held on Saturday afternoon before the prom. Blue linen tablecloths covered the tables, white streamers were draped and taped along the sides and ends of the tables. White menus with blue lettering were printed for the dinner. The diners were given a choice of fried chicken, corn and mashed potatoes with gravy; or baked fish, hush puppies, green beans and french fries. German chocolate cake and apple pie ala'mode were offered as dessert choices. Drinks to be offered were tea, soda or coffee.

We had gotten blue napkins with white lettering imprinted with 'Mt. Pleasant Prom Night 1977'; a boy and girl dancing silhouetted beneath the words. The theme for the prom: 'Time In A Bottle' was printed beneath the silhouette. Programs were also made for the occasion with the same motif, the difference being, the colors were reversed, having blue lettering on white.

The planning committee had decided that a time capsule would also be made commemorating the event which was to include a menu, napkin and program and once they were developed, pictures of the evening. Once the pictures were put into it, the capsule would be sealed, to be opened at their ten year class reunion.

It had been raining for the two days before the prom and we were afraid it would rain on the day of the prom; but the day dawned beautifully, without a cloud in the sky. The dinner and awards ceremony went well, beginning at noon and ending at four o'clock, the seniors received awards for whatever they had been voted most likely to do or be later in life; Ren was voted the most likely to succeed because she was always successful at whatever she chose to do, with Ray being voted to be the most likely to marry Ren. The diners left as soon as the dinner was over so they could get home to begin getting ready for the prom which was set to begin at eight o'clock that night. The servers cleaned the tables off, got everything put back where it belonged, and got the room ready for the evening ahead: then went home to get dressed for the prom.

Ren and I had both bought ankle length halter dresses with long wraps that draped over one arm, then going behind the back, to drape over the other arm; and matching platform shoes. We had decided to use the school colors in our clothing so Ren chose a white dress while I had picked blue. We pinned our long hair up with bobby pins which were covered with long, thin strips of ribbon to keep them from showing; her ribbons were blue, mine white.

Chris wore a white tux so that together, we were blue and white, with Ray wearing a blue one so he and Ren would be blue and white also. When they came to pick us up, the guys told us we looked beautiful, then we all joked with each other about being a walking advertisement for school spirit. We had spent the evening before cleaning out and washing Ray's car so our clothes wouldn't get dirty. Mom, with tears in her eyes, took pictures, and

Jace said senior prom was probably the only reason she would finish high school, because she *really* wanted to go to senior prom; as a senior, that way she could get in on all the fun without having to do any of the work. She got a dirty look from Mom for that comment.

It was dark by the time we reached the school so the blue and white lights along the walkway were twinkling, lighting the way to the evenings festivities. A DJ had been hired for the event and we could hear music coming from the gymnasium as we got out of the car. Walking toward the open doorway we could see the fog from the dry ice drifting through the room.

The long tables had been replaced with smaller, round ones, decorated in the same manner that the larger ones had been, situated around the room near the walls which left a large area in the center for dancing; one long table had been left so we would have someplace to set the punch, glasses and mints. Ballot boxes were placed on each side of the doorway so we could place our votes for King and Queen as we arrived, to be counted after everyone had arrived. About an hour after we arrived, the votes were counted and Prom King and Queen were announced.

Ren and Ray won by a landslide, Chris and I were so proud of them, as was everyone else in the room, judging by the thunderous applause they got as they took the stage to receive their crowns. It was a wonderful night we knew none of us would ever be likely to forget.

Chapter 22

Fighting Evil

Chris '96

Returning from the Abbott's, Chris and I read Kat a story, part of one anyway, because she was too tired to stay awake for all of it. After kissing her good-night and tucking her in, we went down to join the other kids on the patio.

"Dad, did you remember the rodeo is in Mountain Home tomorrow?"

"I'd completely forgotten, Kim. You three have been planning on going for weeks now, haven't you?"

"Yeah, we were wondering if it would be okay if all us kids went, including Kat. If that's alright with you Em."

"Sure, I know you guys will all have fun and Kat's always loved rodeo clowns, so I know she'll enjoy it," I told her, "Besides, the Abbott's are coming over tomorrow and I'd like to be able to get a word in," we all knew that when Kat was around hardly anybody else got a chance to talk. She loved to talk and let everybody know it. "Carrie was my best friend in high school here so we have twenty years to catch up on, *and* she wants your dad and I to explain to them how we ended up with Kat if we haven't seen each other in almost twenty years," I laughed, remembering Carrie saying she wanted the *whole story*.

"Well, it's getting late and we've all got a big day ahead of us tomorrow." Chris said, yawning, "I think I'll go to bed. Good-night all."

"Night Dad," his kids told him.

"Night Chris," my kids said.

"I think I'll go to bed too. Don't stay up too late kids. Kat's gonna be a handful at the rodeo tomorrow, you'll need all the rest you can get." I turned to follow Chris in to the house, "Good-night kids."

"Night Mom."

"Night Em."

As soon as I got up the next morning I began getting everything set out that I would need for our lunch with Carrie and Jared. Chris sent Kim and Chloe in to town to pick up some things he was running low on, potatoes, seasoning salt, eggs and milk. Kat was so excited about the rodeo she could hardly contain herself. She ran around yelling 'ride em cowboy' and 'yippee'! She said she wished her Daddy and I were going but she knew we were having the Abbott's over for dinner and said she guessed it was alright that we weren't going, she knew she was going to have fun with her brothers and sisters.

Jared and Carrie showed up at exactly eleven o'clock. After introducing everyone the older kids ran to get ready for the rodeo. Kat had been ready since she'd been told she was going; which had been when she woke up, so she'd been ready for hours. While the rest of the kids were getting ready she chatted with Carrie and Jared. She talked nonstop until Kim came to let us know the rest of them were ready. Kat hugged Chris and I, shook Carrie and Jared's hands then began pulling Kim toward the front door, eager to get going. She didn't want to wait any longer than she had to, she wanted to go see the clowns.

I trusted the older kids to take care of their sister, so I knew they would be fine at the rodeo. Chris and I reminded them to be careful as they all got into Kim's car and headed for Mountain Home and the rodeo.

We vowed to spend as much of the day as possible NOT talking about the evil surrounding us. We wanted, even if just for a little while, to act like everything was fine and we were just normal people on a normal day, wanting to catch up with old friends.

"OK, spill it." Carrie demanded after the kids had gone, "Where *exactly* did Kat come from?"

I teased her, "It's no wonder you two don't have any kids," I looked over at Jared, "Didn't anybody ever tell her how babies are made?" We all laughed as Carrie's face turned red.

"You know what I mean, Em," she said, when she could stop laughing, "Where did you and Chris see each other again, what? Six … seven ... years ago?"

"We both ended up in Vegas at the same time in '90. I was there to finalize the sale of my first book and he had just bought some more horses. We bumped into each other in front of the hotel."

"And she means that *literally*," Chris put in laughingly, "We were both running to catch the same taxi and almost knocked each other down."

"You're kidding," Jared chuckled. Chris shook his head no, still laughing. "You mean you actually *bumped* into each other."

"Oh yeah, damn near knocked us on our butts, and as we both started to apologize to the person we'd run into we looked at each other and realized who it was we *had* run into. If the look on my face was anything like the look on hers, we both looked like fish out of water," he made a face that was supposed to look shocked, with his mouth opening and closing, "She was standing there with her mouth open, a shocked expression on her face."

"Believe me honey, you looked as much like a guppy as I did," I laughingly told him. "Anyway, our meetings happened to be in the same building so we shared the taxi and made plans to have dinner together that night, which we did. I had originally only planned to be there one or two nights but we ended up spending the next five days together."

"*And* the last four nights," Chris added, smiling, reaching for my hand. Now it was *my turn* to have a red face, "God, I love it when she blushes," he said, reaching out with his free hand to touch my red cheek.

"And here I thought Carrie was the only woman who still blushed," Jared teased. "She hates that she blushes, but I think it's cute." He knew his saying it would cause her to blush and it did. She smiled, knowing there was nothing she could do to stop it from happening.

"Cute," she muttered, "Who wants to be cute at my age."

"It's better than the alternative," Jared patted her on the knee, grinning as he neared the punchline.

"Which is?"

"Bein' ugly. " We all laughed as she playfully swatted at him. "Now, wouldn't you rather be cute?"

"Hell yeah!"

We were having so much fun it was hard to believe there was an evil closing in around us. We had a late lunch and had finished eating before

Jared brought the subject up. We'd filled each other in by then on what we had been up to since we'd all seen each other last. We had known one of us would have to bring it up sooner or later, but I think we were all silently voting for later.

"So Chris, fill us in on what's been happening around here."

Chris told them everything we had learned up to this point. When he finished, it didn't seem to me that we knew near enough about the evil to have any idea how to stop it.

That would soon change.

We spent a few more hours talking about kids, horses, writing, New York and the man with the black eyes. Carrie wanted to see the gazebo, so she and I walked over to it. I found out she had really just wanted to tell me something without the guys hearing. When we rejoined Chris and Jared on the patio, Carrie reminded Jared that they needed to get home, before their dog destroyed the house. He said that while the dog may be a little thing, he didn't like being left alone and when he was he could tear up just as much as a big dog.

We watched them drive away then went back out to the patio. "Today was nice," I said as we sat down on the glider, "relaxing. It was good seeing them again, wasn't it."

"Yeah, it was."

"You'll never believe what Carrie told me when we walked over so she could see the gazebo."

"What?"

"She thinks she might be pregnant!"

"Really?! That's great! They both love kids. I always wondered why they never had any."

"Carrie told me they both want children and they've tried to conceive, she just never got pregnant. The doctors told them it could be because they both had too much stress in their lives due to their demanding jobs, he explained to her that maybe if she could slow down a little, even if she had to force herself to, could spend more time away from work and cut back on the hectic schedule she was keeping, it might help her relax enough to conceive. She told me she thinks it happened after they decided to move back here. She said once the decision was made, she did slow down and relaxed a lot. She hasn't told Jared yet because she didn't want to get his hopes up, just in case she wasn't," I looked at him, "but since she realized today that she's *five weeks* late, the odds are pretty good that she *is* pregnant."

"When will she know?"

"She bought one of those home pregnancy tests in Batesville today and said she was going to use it in the morning, because the paperwork in the box said that's the best time to do it. She said she'd call to let us know, if she was, *after* she told Jared, of course."

"Well, I hope they **are** pregnant," he said.

"I could just *see* Jared being pregnant." I laughed at the idea.

"Oh, you know what I mean," he grinned. Just then, the kids pulled into the driveway.

Kat came running up, "Mommy!! Daddy!! I had so much fun today. I can't wait 'til I get to go to the next rodeo. I didn't like it when they put the ropes on those poor little cows and dragged them down, but I had lots of fun!!"

"They're not called little cows Kat, they're called calves," Joe corrected her.

"Oh well, you knew what I meant, didn't you," she laughed.

"The horses were so pretty Mommy!! Not as pretty as Daddy's horses, but they were pretty. The clowns at the rodeo were even funnier than the last clowns I saw; at the circus," she hugged herself, saying, "I just can't wait 'til the next rodeo!!"

It had been a very big day for Kat and she began yawning, "Chris, you wanna read her a story again tonight?"

"Yeah Daddy, PLEASE?!?! I like it when you read to me." She came over and hugged me, "I like it when you read to me too, Mommy, but Daddy is SO-O-O funny when he reads." She was right about that, he was funny when he read to her.

"Sure, munchkin, go take a bath and brush your teeth, then I'll be up to read you a story. How does that sound?"

"Great, Daddy!!" She hurried off to take her bath. Chloe went with her to keep an eye on her while she was in the tub.

After Kat was gone, Kim said, "Things are getting worse, aren't they Dad?"

"Yes, I'm afraid things are escalating even faster than I first thought they would, Kim," Chris told her, "however, we did find out tonight that the Abbotts have known about what's been going on around here for a long time and they have agreed to help us try to figure out a way to stop it. Once we figure out what *IT* is."

"I thought so, because I remembered what you told us about the spiders and snakes in '71," she shivered, because she disliked both, "First, we saw all those snakes this morning, then tonight on the way home the roads seemed to be covered with tarantulas. Luckily, Kat's too small to be able to see out the car windows so she didn't see them, but she seemed to know they were there Dad; she started singing one of those kids songs, you know, the one about the itsy-bitsy spider. It was really weird Dad, none of us said anything about them being all over the road, and she couldn't see them, so I don't know *how* she knew, but she *knew*. But their being there didn't seem to bother her at all, Em. Chloe told me Kat actually **likes** spiders, tarantulas anyway. I hate them. I think they are disgusting, hairy things."

"Yeah, Kat's a lot like my mom when it comes to tarantulas," I explained, "She's always been fascinated by them, just like my mom. I don't understand how anyone could actually *like* them, they've always given me the creeps; but Kat and my mom both like them."

"There's no accounting for taste, I guess. I don't like 'em either; never have, never will." Chris put in.

Chapter 23

It's Dead, Jim

Both '96

"We got here as soon as we could," Carrie said, ten minutes after I'd hung up the phone to ask for their help. "What's happened? You sounded absolutely frantic when you called. Are the kids all okay?"

"The kids are all fine, so far anyway. We called because we just had a visitor; *two* visitors, actually. Graves brought someone out to meet us. You'll never guess *who* he brought, or *why!*"

"*Who?*"

"*Why?*"

"The man with black eyes. Who's name is Jeffers, by the way. Willard Jeffers, but he prefers to be called Will," I mockingly repeated what he'd told Chris and I more than once.

"Are you *serious*?? What the hell did he want with you?"

Chris shook his head up and down firmly, confirming we were definitely serious, "As serious as a heart attack Carrie! And it isn't **US** he wants!! Oh no, it's not Em and I he wants at all!"

"What *does* he want then?"

"*KAT*!!" Chris and I both said at once.

"Kat? WHY?!?!" They were both shocked. "*W*hat does he want with Kat?!?!"

We repeated what he'd told us as they both sat staring, open mouthed, unable to speak; "That was pretty much our reaction too, mute shock," we told them after we had finished explaining the visit to them.

"Oh my God, we've got to stop him/it, whatever the hell that thing in the pond is! But, I gotta tell ya', I'm at a loss as to exactly how we're gonna do it," Carrie said.

"So are we," Chris admitted.

"Well, we've got to think of something and *fast*!! We don't know how much longer we've got before that thing hatches, or is born or does whatever the hell it has to do to get here. I refuse to let it have my child!! It will have to kill me to get to her!!" I almost yelled.

"We'll come up with a plan, Em, we've just go to try and stay calm."

"Stay CALM?!?! How the hell am I supposed to stay calm when I find out some evil .... *Thing* wants my baby girl?" I realized that I was beginning to get hysterical but was unable to stop it.

Chris pulled me to him and held me close, "We *will* come up with a way to stop it honey, we've just got to think harder."

"I know it's going to be hard to stay calm Em, I'd feel the same way if anything like this ever tried to get my baby," Carrie said, rubbing her stomach. Her home pregnancy test had been positive.

We all sat for a while, each of us silently coming up with ways to kill it in our minds, then discarding our mental plans just as quickly as we came up with them. I was afraid that whatever it was that was in that pond was going to win after all. As soon as that thought came into my mind, I reminded myself that we *were* going to beat it, if only because we had to. We couldn't let it get it's hands, or whatever it had, on Kat.

I finally remembered a story I had heard a long time ago about a small swimming hole in Tennessee that the local kids always used. Occasionally a snake would be seen but not very often; until one day, with the water half full of children, a boy began screaming. The children scrambled out of the water, but by the time they could get the boy who had screamed out of the water, he was dead, snakebites completely covering his body. Apparently the water had become infested with snakes without anyone noticing. The police, debating what to do about the infestation finally decided to hire an expert, who told them that the only way he knew of making sure they got rid of *all* of the snakes was to blow the pond dry with dynamite. Since they were water snakes, if there wasn't any water, the snakes wouldn't have any place to live, (the ones who managed to survive the blast anyway). I told them the story and by the time the kids returned we had decided it was our best, if not only, option.

Jared, who knew two guys from Little Rock who were experts with dynamite *and* who happened to be working at a nearby rock quarry, said he would get in touch with them and ask them to help us do the job. He said we would probably have to pay them a lot of money because what we were planning to do wasn't exactly legal; blowing up a pond on someone else's property., we all agreed we would be willing to pay them almost any amount of money, as long as the job was done; but it would have to be done soon, *very* soon. We decided we should call the two men right away because if we were to have even a small hope of killing the evil that was incubating in the pond, we would have to blow the water out within the next day or two and even that might be too little, too late. We used the speakerphone so we could all be in on the conversation. Jared dialed and we began setting our plan in motion.

"Hello," a mans voice answered the phone at the other end, seeming to echo through the speakerphone.

"Keith? It's Jared, Jared Abbott."

"Hey buddy, long time no see. How the hell are ya man? How's that beautiful wife of yours? Man, you sound like you're right next door, the phone service in New York must be improving," he laughed.

"Actually Keith, I *am* right nest door, in a manner of speaking. Carrie and I began moving back to Mt. Pleasant the end of last week."

"Hi Keith," Carrie cut in, "How have you been?"

"Hey Carrie, nice to hear your voice again. I bet you're just as pretty as ever. You always were a pretty little thing. I wonder if that husband of yours knows how lucky he is?"

"I know Keith, believe me."

"So, Jared, it's been a while now that you guys have finally decided to get smart and drop out of the rat race, maybe we can get together and talk about old times."

"Sure, anytime. Actually we were wondering if you would mind helping us with something, it's right up your alley."

"You mean you want to hire me? To blow something up?"

"That's exactly what I mean. You're the best man for the job," Jared paused, "for two reasons; you're the best dynamite man I know *and* we need someone we can trust, because what we're planning to do isn't *exactly* .... legal."

"What do you guys plan on doing? Blowing somebody away?" He joked, but we could tell by his voice that he was half serious.

Nothing quite that extreme, Keith. We just want to blow a pond dry that is on someone else's property."

"Why? Did the owner piss you off or something?" Keith teased him.

"I wish it were that simple man. We're doing it because the pond has become infested with snakes, really aggressive snakes; one child has died already and we're not going to let it happen again. The only way we know to get rid of the snakes altogether is to destroy their home. We figure no water, no snakes."

"Man, I'm sorry. That's awful, poor kid. I didn't mean to sound so callous. Sounds serious."

"Hey it's okay, you didn't know. But, it *is* serious."

Chris whispered to me that he wanted to ask Keith some questions, so I touched Jared's shoulder and let him know. "Hey Keith, some friends of ours, Chris and Em, are in on this with us, as a matter of fact, we're calling from their place. They want to ask you a few questions, if you don't mind."

"Sure man, any friend of yours is a friend of mine."

"Hello Keith, this is Chris. We were wondering, if you did decide to do the job, how much would it cost. We've never done anything like this before so we have no idea what expenses we'll have."

"Well, it sounds like a two man job, and dynamite don't come cheap, especially for jobs that aren't , as Jared put it, 'exactly legal', so I figure ten thousand dollars for each man should cover it. Hold on, I'll ask my partner if he'd mind doing the job with me," he must have covered the phone with his hand because we could hear muffled voices coming from the speakerphone.

Finally, "Jack said he'll help me with it but he doesn't think we can get to it for three or four days."

We need it done sooner than that, so I broke into the conversation, "Keith, this is Em. We know you will both be risking a lot so we're willing to pay you each twenty five thousand dollars, if you can do it tomorrow."

Keith whistled, "Just a sec, let me talk to Jack again," he covered the phone again, returning a few moments later, "Jack said for that kind of money, we can make the time."

"Thank you Keith, you have no idea how much we appreciate this. It's very important that we get it done tomorrow, that's the only way we can be absolutely sure it doesn't happen to anyone else's child," the other three nodded their agreement, "I'll let you speak to Jared again, he can give you directions on how to get here. Thank you so much."

Jared gave them directions to Chris' and Keith told us that he and Jack would be at Chris' by eight thirty the next morning. Now that we had a plan to destroy the evil, we all relaxed a little and spent the rest of the evening talking about everything *BUT* it. Carrie and Jared left around ten thirty, saying they would see us in the morning. I would go to the nearest bank first thing in the morning and get fifty thousand dollars transferred from my bank to pay Keith and Jack.

By ten o'clock the next morning we were all at Bailey's Pond. The plan was that we would pay the two men before we ever left Chris' house; then when we got to Bailey's Pond, Keith and Jack were to place the charges while Chris and I guarded the road to the West of the pond, with Jared and Carrie guarding the East road in their four wheel drive truck. After the charges were placed, with a ten minute timer on them, we would all get as far away as we could while still being able to guard the roads leading to it.

Carrie and Jared and the two men would go to the first mile road East and wait, with Chris and I going West to the end of the driveway by the stop sign.

It was the longest ten minutes of my life. Nine minutes and fifty-eight seconds into it Chris and I reached out for each other's hands, looked directly at where the blast would be occurring and prayed it would work. Two minutes passed, then the ground shook as the dynamite detonated. We could see what looked like a wall of water shoot up into the air, then felt droplets of it hit the truck, the ditches on both sides of the road quickly began filling up as the dam broke, causing the stream coming from the pond to overflow. We waited five more minutes, then drove toward the pond to make sure what we'd set out to do had been accomplished.

When we reached the pond we could see it had no water left in it at all, the only thing it contained was a large, multi veined, womb like sac that resembled a large balloon that was slowly deflating; which looked as if it contained a child sized human like being.

It had worked!! The evil that had been incubating in the pond in the womb like amniotic sac for the past twenty five years seemed to be dying, just as it was about to be born.

Carrie and Jared pulled up beside us as Chris, ever the Trekkie, joked, "It's Dead Jim!" We laughed, at his joke as well as in relief that our plan had worked. "Now let's all get the hell out of here, before somebody comes to investigate the blast." We all agreed with him and hurried away from the scene.

The child like shape had all but ceased it's struggles as we hurried to reach the highway West of the pond. In our haste we didn't see the car barreling down the road toward the pond from the East, nor did it see us. We were just pulling onto the highway as Jeffers jumped from the car and ran to the deflating sac, managing to pull a fully formed, seven year old male child of approximately seven years old from it, just as it collapsed completely.

Chapter 24

Lost Love

Em '76

School, in the days following the prom were hectic; filled with a flurry of finals, plans for graduation and summer vacation, picking classes for the next school year, and the seniors completing and mailing their college applications.

Chris and I were happy we got all of our junior classes together. Ren and Ray applied to the same colleges, both having good grades, they got accepted at most of them. They decided on a school in New York because it had the best curriculum for what they wanted. They had decided to become attorneys. I couldn't believe they were going to be so far away.

Jace had finally made it to high school and was excited even though she had gone from being an upperclassman in junior high to being low man on the totem pole in high school. She was now one year closer to being a senior, one year closer to getting out of school altogether. At the time, that seemed to be her *only* goal in life.

Graduation was two weeks before the last day of school for the rest of us. The time seemed to fly by and soon graduation was over, then the next two weeks were gone and we were free for the summer.

Ren, Ray, Chris and I spent that summer much the way we had the one before; working hard and playing harder. Again we hauled hay, caught chickens, tilled and planted fields and worked in the sawmill. Knowing what to expect this time, Ren and I had an easier time doing them than we had the year before. We did spend a little less time working that summer than we had the one before however, because we knew Ren and Ray would be going off to college in New York in the fall and we wanted to have all the fun we could before they left. Chris and I knew we would miss having them to hang out with, but consoled ourselves with the knowledge that at least we would be together after they'd gone.

The three months of that summer seemed to be as short as the three months our family had spent in the camper in Batesville had seemed long. All too soon, it was time for Ren and Ray to go off to college and Chris and I to return to high school. For the next month, Chris and I were inseparable, the only time we were apart was when we each had to go home at night to sleep. We hated being separated for any reason.

Then, one day in September, Mom told us the branch of the company Dad worked for was closing and we were going to have to return to Kansas so he could work in the branch office there.

Crying, I told Chris the awful news. We tried to talk my parents into letting me stay, with no luck. I was forced to go with them, leaving Chris behind.

Chapter 25

Livin' Large

Both '96

In the weeks following the destruction of Bailey's Pond, we kept a close eye on events in the area. A sense of humor began returning to the town, the people stopped being so suspicious of newcomers, the cattle returned to normal and could be eaten without fear of being 'infected' by it, although most of the town decided they didn't care much for eating beef once they began being able to think for themselves again. Best of all, the snake population dropped dramatically, quickly returning to normal within a few days of the blast.

It was nice to see people laughing and happy to be alive again, especially for Chris; he had lived with the non-caring, non-feeling, lemming-like people for most of his life and was glad they were finally acting human again.

Some of the people decided to move from the area once they could think for themselves again; saying it wasn't that they didn't *like* it around there, it was just that they had remained simply because they had no choice in the matter, they *couldn't* leave before now.

Carrie and Jared had decided they were not returning to New York but were going to remain in the old home place because it was a better environment to raise children in. The biggest crime we had in the area was teen-agers hot-rodding up and down the road in front of the school and doing donuts in it's parking lot with their vehicles.

A month after the explosion at Bailey's Pond, my kids and I were still at Chris', having made no plans to return to our home in Kansas. Kat was enjoying the opportunity to get to know her Dad and new brother and sisters; JJ had bought himself a 4X4 truck and was having a ball driving on all the dirt roads and hills in the surrounding countryside; Chloe and CJ had grown almost as close to each other as Chris and I had been years earlier and Joe liked being able to go out on the lake behind the house in Chris' speedboat.

"I don't think you're ever going to get your kids to agree to leave Em," Chris told me one evening as we sat on the patio, watching Joe and CJ zipping back and forth across the lake in the speedboat.

"I've been thinking the same thing," I said, as I reached out to take his hand in mine, "I've also been wondering if that would be such a bad thing." I was watching him out of the corner of my eye, trying to gauge his reaction to my remark.

A questioning look in his eye, he turned to me, "Are you trying to say you're thinking of staying?" He asked, hopefully.

"If you'd like us to."

"*If I'd like you to*?!?! I've been wondering how to ask you to stay, wondering what the kids would say if I asked you to marry me."

"*MARRY YOU?*" I had waited so long to hear him ask me that, I couldn't believe it was finally happening.

"Yes Em, marry me. I've loved you since that day in front of the general store, all those years ago. If your family hadn't moved away, I was planning to ask you to marry me after we graduated. I hated being away from you all those years. I married Alyssa simply because I wanted children," he saw the look on my face, "Oh, I loved her, in a way, but I've *never* felt about anyone else the way I've always felt about you. I thought it was going to kill me when your family suddenly left that summer."

"I know the feeling, I wanted to die. I was angry at my parents for years because they made me go with them. But when the company Dad worked for closed because that guy embezzled all the money, we had no choice. Remember, we tried to talk them into letting me stay, but you know how that went. Then came college, and Jake. We had a happy enough marriage, considering we got married in the first place because we weren't careful enough and I got pregnant with JJ and Chloe. But I never forgot the times you and I were together and sometimes I let it cause problems in my marriage by taking my anger at my parents for having made me leave you out on my husband. If he hadn't died in that plane crash we probably would have ended up getting divorced anyway, because I never felt about him the way I've always felt about you. I *loved him*, but I wasn't *in love with him;* the only person I felt *both* for was you, and he knew it."

"It was pretty much the same way with my marriage to Alyssa. She knew I was still in love with you and she dealt with it the best she could, but it still caused problems occasionally. We had a reasonably happy marriage, but she knew I would rather have been with you." He pulled my hand to his lips and kissed my fingertips, "I never stopped loving you Em. *NEVER!*"

"And I never stopped loving you Chris."

"So you'll stay?"

"I'll talk to the kids today when I get the chance and see what they think, but I'm sure they'll agree we belong here. They know how you and I have always felt about each other and they want me to be happy. You make me happy and they realize it. I don't think they'll have a problem with staying here, *or* with you and I getting married."

"I take it that's a yes."

"Yes, it's a yes," he pulled me close, sealing the bargain with a kiss.

"Does this mean what I hope it means?" Chloe and Kim asked in unison as they came out onto the patio in time to hear the last part of our conversation.

Chris grinned, "I don't know, just what do you hope it means?"

"That you two have decided to *finally* get married!" JJ laughed as he came around the side of the house. He had apparently heard the last part of our conversation too, as well as the question Kim and Chloe had asked. "It's about time."

"So you guys would be alright with that?" I asked, as they sat down. "We would like it if you were all OK with our decision."

"Alright?!?!?! It's *GREAT*!!!" They said, all at the same time, their enthusiasm causing us all to laugh. JJ and Chloe said they had been debating whether or not *I* could be talked into staying and they were glad they weren't going to have to try; Kim said it would be nice having a mom again.

"Kids! You never know how they'll react," Chris joked, throwing his hands in the air.

By then, the rest of the kids had made their way to the patio; CJ and Joe from the lake, Kari had just finished reading a book and Kat from her nap.

We filled them in on our plans and they were all *more than happy* with the idea, *especially* Kat, because it meant she would get to have a Mommy *and* a Daddy for the first time in her life.

We had discussed it and decided we would never tell Kat about the evil or what it had wanted. We hoped that what she didn't know, couldn't hurt her.

Chapter 26

A New Evil Begins

Kat 2011

"Em, honey, phone," Chris called from the kitchen, "It's Kat, she wants to talk to both of us."

After glancing at the serene lake again, I got up to go into the house to talk to our daughter on the phone. She had gone off to college in California after graduating high school and was due home for spring break in two weeks. I hoped she wasn't calling to say she couldn't make it.

"Mom, Dad," I heard after she knew I'd picked up the extension, "I was going to wait until I came home for break to tell you but I just *had* to tell you now!" Even as an adult, she put all her energy into her voice, seeming to punctuate every sentence with an exclamation point.

"Tell us what, hon?"

"I met the greatest guy in the whole world! He's gorgeous Mom!! I can't wait for you guys to meet him! I'm bringing him home with me at break."

"That serious huh?" Chris joked. Kat was always falling for some gorgeous guy or another.

"Oh Dad, he's just wonderful. I just know you and Mom will love him as much as I do!" She paused to catch her breath, then continued, "I hope so anyway, because we plan to get married as soon as we can!"

"We'll talk about the marriage part when you get home Kat." 'MARRIED??' I mouthed silently to Chris, "For now, we'll settle for knowing what this wonderful, gorgeous guy looks like."

"He's six feet tall, about a hundred and ninety five pounds, blonde hair; and I swear Mom, BLACK EYES!!!"

"OH MY GOD!! *NO-O-O*!!!!" I screamed. Chris caught me just as my knees buckled.

Other Books By Mickey Stroda:
'Blood Ties ~ The Beginning'

'Flight of the Raven' – with Amanda Rhodes

'Del Lind Destiny' – as Belle Fairchild

'Season To Season ~ A Family Poetry Potpourri' - Mickey (Bell) Stroda, Lucille
Bell, Reney (Bell) Turner, Kristi (Bell) Rhodes, Sara Stroda and Amanda Rhodes

* * * *

Other Published Works By Mickey Stroda:

Inclusions in Anthologies:

Remley Literary Agency;

God's Smallest Angels - in 'In His Hands' in 1999

* * * *

The American Poetry Association:

A Love To Call My Own - in ' The Poetry Of Life' in 1987

* * * *

The Poetry Guild:

And Me - in 'Shelter From The Storm' in 1998

* * * *

Famous Poets Society:

Tears For Oklahoma - in 'A Treasury Of Great Poems - Famous Best Poems Of
1998' in 2000

* * * *

International Library Of Poetry Anthologies:

''The Poetry of Life' in 1987

'The Mystical Night'' in 1999

'The Window Of Remembrance' in 2000

'Nature's Echoes' in 2000
* * * *

Imprint Books Anthologies
'Barn and Snow' in 2001

Mickey Stroda

Mickey Stroda writes full-time. She has published poems in numerous anthologies, including 'The Poetry of Life' and 'Words Of Praise' in 1987, 'Shelter From The Storm' in 1998, 'Yesterday and Tomorrow', 'The Silence Remembers', 'In His Hands' in 1999, 'A Treasury Of Great Poems', 'The Window Of Remembrance' and 'Nature's Echoes' in 2000 and 'Barn and Snow' in 2001, among many others.

Ms. Stroda has previously had this book, Blood Ties, as well a her first novel, Bailey's Pond, published by Bookbooters.com, who are now out of business. Both are now available here at Lulu.com. A series of collections of poetry, are also available at Lulu.com, as well as a number of other books in a variety of genres. At present, she is working on the second book in the Blood Ties series. She plans to have at least six books in the series.

She recently finished a young adult novel, Flight of the Raven, which was co-written with her eleven-year-old niece, Amanda Rhodes. They plan to make the novel part of a series of young adult books. They are now working on the next book in the Raven series, which is to be titled Raven in the Middle. She also has a variety of other projects she is working on, which include two science fiction novels, a couple of mystery/detective novels and some children/teen stories.

She has also begun writing a series of romance novels under the pseudonym Belle Fairchild. She plans to call the series 'Desire in the Heartland', which will all take place in Kansas. The first of these romance novels is called Del Lind Destiny and is currently listed at Lulu.com. She is working on her next romance novel, it is called A Fair To Remember.

Mickey lives in Kansas. She can be emailed at msstroda@yahoo.com.